Every Voice Ain't From God

A Christian Romance Thriller

TANISHA STEWART

Every Voice Ain't From God: A Christian Romance Thriller
Copyright © 2022 Tanisha Stewart

All rights reserved.

Every Voice Ain't From God: A Christian Romance Thriller is a work of fiction. Any resemblance to events, locations, or persons living or dead is coincidental. No part of this book may be reproduced in any written, electronic, recording, or photocopying form without written permission of the author, Tanisha Stewart.

Books may be purchased in quantity and for special sales by contacting the publisher, Tanisha Stewart, at tanishastewart.author@gmail.com.

Editing: Cynful Monarch
cynfulmonarch.com

Cover Design: Carrie Bledsoe
hello@thecarriecompany.com

First Edition
Published in the United States of America
by Tanisha Stewart

Table of Contents

Chapter 1 1
Chapter 2 4
Chapter 3 7
Chapter 4 11
Chapter 5 14
Chapter 6 16
Chapter 7 19
Chapter 8 22
Chapter 9 25
Chapter 10 28
Chapter 11 31
Chapter 12 35
Chapter 13 38
Chapter 14 41
Chapter 15 44
Chapter 16 48
Chapter 17 52
Chapter 18 54
Chapter 19 58
Chapter 20 61
Chapter 21 64
Chapter 22 66
Chapter 23 69
Chapter 24 72

Chapter 25 75
Chapter 26 78
Chapter 27 83
Chapter 28 86
Chapter 29 90
Chapter 30 94
Chapter 31 98
Chapter 32 104
Chapter 33 107
Chapter 34 109
Chapter 35 112
Chapter 36 117
Chapter 37 120
Chapter 38 125
Chapter 39 129
Chapter 40 133
Chapter 41 136
Chapter 42 138
Chapter 43 141
Chapter 44 143
Chapter 45 146
Chapter 46 149
Chapter 47 151
Chapter 48 154
Chapter 49 158

Chapter 50 161
Chapter 51 164
Chapter 52 168
Chapter 53 172
Chapter 54 174
Chapter 55 180
Chapter 56 184
Chapter 57 187
Chapter 58 191
Chapter 59 194
Chapter 60 199
Chapter 61 201
Chapter 62 205
Chapter 63 211
Chapter 64 214
Chapter 65 219
Chapter 66 224
Chapter 67 226
Chapter 68 228
Chapter 69 231
Chapter 70 234

Dear Reader,

I hope you enjoy this Christian romance thriller. Once you finish the story, I would love it if you left a review. Not sure what to say? It's fine – just comment on the characters or your overall thoughts on the book (**no spoilers, please!**).

Pressed for time? You can leave a star rating (1 = low; 5 = high). Either way, I would love to hear from you. I read all reviews left for my books and often use the feedback to improve future releases. Not to mention, reader reviews help authors keep going!

Lastly, if you would like to connect with me, feel free to join my reader's group, Tanisha Stewart Readers, on Facebook, or my email list at www.tanishastewartauthor.com/contact.

I look forward to hearing your thoughts and interacting with you!

Tanisha Stewart

From the Back Cover

A psychological thriller with jaw-dropping twists and turns, and characters whose antics will leave you speechless... A story about love gone right, then wrong.

Zakari has known Nicole was **the one** since high school. He prays about whether their relationship is meant to be and receives confirmation one night during a church service. Zakari and Nicole are getting married!

Until **she breaks up with him** the next day.

Zakari plunges into a pit of despair, then Nicole reaches out and tells him they can be friends, maybe rekindle their relationship after college? Elated, Zakari agrees and bides his time until **he and Nicole can be together** again.

But Nicole gets **engaged to another man**, and Zakari doesn't understand.

He and Nicole are meant to be - she just needs to see it.

And **her fiancé needs to be eliminated**.

Every Voice Ain't From God is a twisted and page-turning tale about a man who will stop at nothing to have his woman's heart. **Including murder.**

Acknowledgements

I would like to give a very special shout out to the woman who inspired this read.

One day, T. Lynn Gray, poet and author of Hindsight: A Book of Poetry and Prose, shared with me a story about a relationship gone wrong, a love triangle that was forged as a result of someone believing they had heard from God, and as she spoke, the wheels began turning for this story. Zakari and Nicole were born.

Thank you!

Every Voice Ain't From God

Chapter 1

Zakari

I had been thinking about Nicole all day, but she hadn't called me back yet.

Oh, right, she was at work. She did tell me that. I needed to call her now since she was probably off. I went to her name in my contacts and pressed Call, my heart fluttering the entire time. The phone rang eight times and went to voicemail at first, but when I called again, she answered on the third ring. "Hello?"

I relaxed. "Hey, babe! How was work?"

"Um, it was good. What did you do today?"

I played with my collar. "Nothing, just sit here and think of you."

She giggled. "Boy, that's all you say you ever do."

I put some bass in my tone. Nicole loved my sexy voice. "Come on, little mama. You know I can't get you off my mind."

She giggled again. "Zakari, you are such a trip."

"Want to hang out today?" I blurted out.

"Tonight? Hm, let me see if my mom wants me to do something. Hold on, I'll call you back."

We hung up, and I waited by my phone for her to call back, but she must have forgotten like she did the last three times. After about a half hour, I called her again.

"Hello?" she answered like she was in the middle of something.

"Hey, silly. Did you forget about me?"

Nicole was silent. "Oh, no, remember I told you I was going to ask my mom if she wanted me to do something?"

"Yes."

"She asked me to clean out the backyard. Sorry, I can't hang out tonight."

"Oh, that's fine, babe. Want me to come over and help? We could knock it out together."

There was more silence before she said, "Zakari, that's so sweet. Sure, come on over."

"No problem! On my way." I changed into some sweats and a wife beater so Nicole could see my muscles, then hopped in my car to head to Nicole's mom's house. Her and Nicole's dad got divorced a few years back, and Nicole was sad. When we first met, she opened up to me about it. I was her shoulder to cry on for the whole thing, and now, two years later, we were going places. Marriage and kids, I hoped. We just had to get through college first.

I pulled up to Nicole's house ready to work. She gave me a brief hug then handed me a huge black trash bag. I held it open while she threw various items in it, from leaves to old boots to miscellaneous things like candy wrappers. We filled the bag, then went to work on her mother's garden, making sure all the flowers and vegetables were watered. I snuck and pulled a flower while Nicole wasn't looking, then gave it to her when she turned back to me. She smiled and put it behind her ear.

"You look pretty like that," I said.

"Thank you." Her expression changed from a smile to a more neutral look. "Zakari…" she started, but her mom came down the back steps with two big glasses of lemonade.

"Look at you two, peas in a pod!" she said, handing one glass to me and the other to Nicole. "Y'all finished already?"

"Yes, Ma'am," I answered.

"We got to keep you around, Zakari!" she commented, and it warmed my heart.

We drank our lemonade, then went inside for dinner.

Chapter 2

Nicole

I had been trying to find a way to get rid of Zakari for a while.

It wasn't that he was a bad guy, it was that college was looming. I didn't want to be in a long-distance relationship while trying to build my future. My mom loved Zakari, and so did my best friend, Shareese, but he wasn't it for me, I knew it. Maybe once we graduated and were ready to settle down, but right now? I was only seventeen for God's sake.

"Nicole!" Mom called me. I went running to her room.

"Yes, Ma?"

"You got your outfit ready for tomorrow?" Tomorrow was church.

"Yes, Ma."

"Good. Iron this blouse for me, please?" She handed me a blouse that already looked straight enough. I had half a mind to ask her why she didn't iron it herself, but I didn't. I was trying to keep all my teeth.

I wordlessly left her room and went to the pantry to grab the iron and board. Once I finished, she handed me her skirt, too.

"Ma, can I ask you something?" I couldn't help it.

"Yes?" She turned around to face me with her hand on one hip.

"Why are you always making me do things you could be doing yourself?"

HOLLAND, RAVIN R
66864

Friday, May 16, 2025

3118321711301S   Every voice ain't from Go

R RAVIN, HOLLAND
49884

Friday, May 16, 2025

She assessed me with her eyes. "Things like what?"

I was a little nervous and hoped she wouldn't get mad at me for asking, but since we were here, I did it. "Like your laundry, and the dishes, and even cooking sometimes."

"I'm preparing you for adulthood. Plus, you're about to go live in the dorms. I'll be out of your hair soon enough."

Those words seemed to satisfy her, and she turned back around and resumed her trek back up the stairs to her bedroom.

I finished ironing her outfit, then decided to go ahead and do mine, too. I guessed helping out around the house wasn't so bad after all.

Later that night, Zakari called me, but I didn't answer. I was hoping he would sense me pulling back and come out and ask what was wrong, but he never did. I knew it was a punk way out, but I didn't want to hurt his feelings. The problem was, no matter how many phone calls I ignored or how much disinterest I showed in his conversation, he never caught the hint.

I shared my feelings with Shareese, and she said I should just tell him, but I didn't know how. Plus, Shareese probably wasn't the best one to give advice, anyway, since she never even had a man.

That probably sounded harsh, but it was the truth. My mom always told me to never ask your friends who didn't have a man for advice about your man. I wasn't sure if that advice worked for her, seeing that she didn't have a man, either, but she and my dad were married for most of my life, so it must have counted for something.

I hung my outfit up and stared at myself in the mirror.

A smile crossed my features as I thought of how college would be. No more parents telling me what to do, waking up and going to sleep when I felt like it, and all kinds of parties and fun to get into. My mom didn't allow me to do much but church here at home.

At college, I would be far away from her prying eyes...

A call from Shareese buzzed on my bed, breaking me out of my thoughts.

"Hello?"

"Girrrrl," she said, rolling her r's like always.

"What is it?" I asked, already about to laugh because I knew it was something stupid.

"Let me tell you," she started, then launched into her latest story of what kind of drama she and her coworkers cooked up that day.

Chapter 3

Zakari

My mom said I should get a summer job so I could save money for college. I went ahead and applied because it was always good for a man to have money. I definitely wanted to be a provider for Nicole.

If a man didn't work, he didn't eat. That was what Pastor always said.

I couldn't wait for Nicole to come to my church. I had been trying to get her to visit for a while, and one time she did, but I didn't think she liked it. Probably because Elder White was preaching. Elder White was long-winded at times, so I could understand why Nicole didn't like his preaching. She would definitely like Prophet Lincoln, though. He came to our church every July to preach a revival, and this year would be no different.

I loved when he came because he always had a prophecy for everyone in the building. Some people didn't appreciate his style, but Pastor said the Lord used people in different ways, so who were we to judge? I certainly wasn't judging.

I hoped Prophet Lincoln had a prophecy for me this year because I had been asking God about a few things. The main thing was Nicole. Was she gonna be my wife or what? I felt in my heart that she was, and I even looked up houses online we could buy together once we got married. I had a list of names we could give our kids, too. Just suggestions, though. Nicole would definitely have a say-so. Pastor always said the husband and wife should both have a say-so in the marriage.

One of the job applications I filled out went through. They called me for an interview the same day. I took it as a sign. I needed to start saving money if I was serious about my future with Nicole.

I went to the interview, and the hiring manager asked me easy questions. Silly ones, too. *Would I ever steal from the cash register?* Of course not! *What would I do if a customer yelled at me?* Smile and give them what they wanted, duh. The customer was always right, everybody knew that.

After that boring interview, I got the job. I was going to make two dollars above minimum wage. I thought the hiring manager liked me because I said I was headed to college. Too bad I wouldn't be able to continue at the store once I was gone.

Oh well, time to call Nicole.

I texted her before the interview, but she didn't text back. She had been really absentminded lately. She must have been worried about college. Maybe I could take her out somewhere nice tonight with money from my allowance.

I laughed so hard when my parents said I would be cut off from allowance when my paychecks started rolling in. I guessed that was fair enough. The allowance wasn't much, anyway. Plus, I was looking forward to making my own money. Nicole's paychecks were huge. Like two hundred dollars a week. Sometimes three. I was about to be rolling in dough, just like her.

The date tonight was a good idea. I would help take Nicole's mind off college and us being away from each other, and we could also celebrate my new job. Nicole already had a job. My woman was so smart. She already had lots of money saved.

I called her on my Bluetooth on my way home from the interview.

"Hello?" she answered.

I perked up at the sound of her voice. I always did. I could never get enough of Nicole. "Hey, lady!"

"Zakari, are you driving?"

I tensed. "Yes…"

There was a sternness to her tone with the next words she spoke. "You know your mom said you shouldn't talk on the phone while driving. I wouldn't want to get you in trouble."

That straightened me right up. "Okay, I'll call back once I get home."

We hung up.

I turned down my street with a chuckle. Nicole was going to be the best wife ever. She was always looking out for me like she just did. Making sure I wasn't distracted while driving. I couldn't wait for her to have my babies.

I pulled into the driveway of my parent's house, then made sure I was fully in park before I called Nicole back. Last time, I got too excited and almost hit the front steps. Good thing I had quick reflexes.

"Hello?" she answered.

"I'm home."

"Great."

I waited a beat, then held back my excitement as I launched into the reason for my call. "Hey, I wanna ask you something. Actually, two things."

"What is it?"

"First, did you want to come to the revival at my church next week? Prophet Lincoln is preaching."

"Um… sure, that's fine. What's the second thing?"

My heart leapt with anticipation when she agreed to see Prophet Lincoln. "The second thing is, I wanted to know if you wanted to go out tonight. We can celebrate me getting a new job and help take your mind off college. I know you've been worried."

Nicole was silent for a moment. "Sure, that's fine. We can go out."

"Great! I'll pick you up at seven."

I hung up and went in the house to get myself together. Nicole and I were going to have a blast.

Chapter 4

Nicole

I was dreading this date with Zakari tonight. At the same time, I agreed to go because I didn't want to hurt his feelings. I needed to find a way to tell him it was over between us, but I didn't know how. The days were flying by, and summer would be over before we knew it. Zakari and I were going to different colleges, which would make the breakup a lot easier, but I knew it would be completely wrong to not tell him until the last minute, or worse, go off to college and tell him then.

I also didn't want to go to the revival at his church, but I agreed to that too because I didn't want to hurt his feelings. To cut to the chase, Zakari's church was weird. The preacher was always going on about *shifting seasons* and *changing atmospheres*, and the people shouted *Amen* at everything he said, even if he wasn't really saying anything. I loved church, but Zakari's church's style wasn't for me. Maybe it was because we were part of different denominations. My mom said people who were part of different denominations sometimes viewed the Bible differently.

All I knew was that my denomination seemed to make the Bible clearer and easier to understand, whi¹ Zakari's church, the preacher mentioned a script never went back to it his whole sermon. M⸱ being too harsh. I did only go to his chu⸱ after all. Maybe the elder who preache⸱

and forgot to get back to the scriptures. I didn't know. It wasn't like I was a preacher myself.

Maybe I would go to this revival with an open mind, give the church a fair chance, then break up with Zakari.

I burst out laughing at that thought. Not that it was funny but because there was no easy way to do what needed to be done.

I had half a mind to call Shareese and see if she would go to the revival with us. Shareese didn't go to church that much. Her mom took her sometimes, but her dad was a Jehovah's Witness. Because of that, she often got confused about which side to believe. I told her Christianity was right, but I didn't think she heard me, because for one, I wasn't a preacher, and two, she wasn't necessarily torn between belief systems, she was torn between her parents. They fought over her, and I knew it had to be hard. I tried to be there for her the best I could, but I could only do so much.

I knew Shareese would be even happier than me when she went off to college. Once she was away from her parents, she would be able to have a clear mind without their interference. Unfortunately, me and Shareese wouldn't get to go to the same school. That was our dream, but I got accepted to my reach school, and she didn't. She got accepted to our second choice. I loved my best friend, but I didn't want to give up my dream school for her.

I hoped that wasn't a bad decision, because I would miss her. On the other hand, if either of our schools turned out to be a bad fit, we could always transfer.

A wave of fear and anxiety passed over me at the thought of being away from everyone I knew. I was probably just being dramatic because thousands of students did it every year, but still. I loved my mom, I loved Shareese, and even Zakari wasn't all bad.

I hoped I was making the right choice.

Chapter 5

Zakari

I had been counting down the days to the revival all week.

I started my new job, and it was going well. The hiring manager liked me because I learned quickly and was even helping some of the older employees with the new cash register. I explained it in a way that Miss Roberta could understand, and she stopped making mistakes and cashed her customers out a lot quicker.

"Zakari, we need to keep you around," Zena, the hiring manager said. "You sure you don't want to switch colleges?"

We shared a laugh after that. "Sorry, I'm only here for the rest of the summer, but we can certainly work out a deal for next year!"

Zena smiled and gave me a nod, then continued with the inventory. The rest of my shift was boring. I made small talk with Miss Roberta, helped tidy up a few of the aisles, and counted the moments until I could go free.

As soon as I got out, I called Nicole.

"Hello?" she answered.

"Hey, sweet thang!"

"Hey, Zakari."

I picked up a sense of irritation in her tone. "What's wrong?"

"Nothing."

I waited for her to continue or to snap out of her mood, but she didn't say anything else, so I continued.

"You off work?"

She sighed. "Yup."

"Wanna hang out?"

"Zakari, I..."

"What is it?" I sat at attention. This didn't sound too good. I hoped everything was okay with her.

"Nothing."

"You sure? Whatever it is, you can tell me. You know I'm here for you."

"I know."

"So, what is it?"

"It's nothing, for real. Where are you headed?" She sounded more upbeat now, so I allowed myself to relax.

I smiled. "Hopefully to see my pretty lady."

She giggled. "Don't you get tired of seeing me every day?"

"Never. Absence makes the heart grow fonder. Every time we leave each other, I count down the moments until we can see each other again."

Nicole fell silent again.

"Nicole?"

"Yeah?"

"You sure everything is okay?"

"Yeah, I was just stretching. Let me change out of my work clothes so I can be ready for you when you get here."

"Okay, great." I hung up and clicked my seatbelt, then turned the car on to exit the parking lot. On the way there, my mind went to the upcoming revival. I sure hoped Prophet Lincoln had a word for me.

Chapter 6

Nicole

I was going to tell him, but I froze like I always did.

This breakup was going to be a lot harder than I thought. Zakari took me to the movies that night, but I paid for everything out of guilt. He kept insisting that he had it, but I made up an excuse about wanting to do something nice for him since he got his new job.

"Thanks, babe," he said with a huge grin, and I almost died.

Zakari wasn't a bad guy. It was me who was the problem. He had been nothing but good to me since we got together. He listened when I cried countless times about my parent's divorce, he helped me with tough homework assignments for my math class, and he was always there to support and encourage me whenever I felt down or was excited about an accomplishment.

I did similar things for him, too, it was just...

What was it? Was I shallow?

From all the books I read, and TV shows I watched, people would likely call me stupid for wanting to break things off with such a good guy.

Despite knowing that, I still wanted things to be over between us. It wasn't that I wasn't attracted to him, half the girls at school were. It wasn't that we didn't have chemistry, we always did. Maybe it was the idea of a long-distance relationship that was weighing me down.

Zakari and I would be hundreds of miles apart, each of us getting a fresh start at a new school.

"Maybe we can take a break for college and get back together afterward..." I said to myself in the mirror.

The doorbell rang. Zakari was here.

Tonight, we were going to the revival at his church. I promised myself I was going to go with an open mind, but my heart wasn't in it.

I shook my shoulders and forced a smile on my face to reset my mood, then went downstairs.

"Hey!" I greeted him with a hug and kiss on the cheek.

Zakari was looking good. He was always sexy in his church attire. He had his fancy shiny shoes with black slacks, a white shirt, and maroon suspenders with a matching bowtie. What was I thinking, letting go of a heartthrob like that?

"You look beautiful," he said with a smile.

See? He was charming, too. I needed to get myself checked. Something was clearly wrong with me for letting him go. We walked hand in hand to his car, then he opened the door for me and gave a playful bow after opening the passenger side door.

I sat inside, and he closed it behind me, then went around to his side to hop in.

"Ready to roll?" he asked. When I nodded, he put his arm over the back of my seat and craned his neck to look behind him for cars.

We pulled out of the driveway, and I contemplated once again whether I was making the right decision.

When we pulled up to the church, the parking lot was already full. This was a change from the time I visited Zakari's church before. That had to be a good sign for this Prophet Lincoln character Zakari was always raving about.

We found a space in the jam-packed lot, then walked hand in hand inside the church. The sanctuary was abuzz with excitement as Zakari smiled and greeted his church family. I smiled and greeted them too, even though I didn't know any of them.

Zakari and I found a seat in the back and waited for the service to begin.

Chapter 7

Zakari

My heart was pounding nonstop since Nicole and I entered the sanctuary.

I spotted Prophet Lincoln as him and Pastor entered the pulpit from Pastor's office, which was situated behind it.

He glanced out into the crowd, and I swore we caught eyes. We did. He winked and waved at me, and I winked and waved back. That was the moment I knew this was going to be my night. Prophet Lincoln had a word for me.

The service started not too long after that. Mother Williams got up and sang and tore the house down. I almost forgot Nicole was there with me, but when I glanced over at her, she was standing and clapping, too. I knew she would like my church.

The praise team sang a few songs back-to-back, then it slowed down for the worship session.

Brother Sinclair came up to lead the worship, and his smooth, baritone voice filled the atmosphere. Eyes were bowed, hands were raised, and voices were singing and shouting to the Lord.

It was beautiful, and I was caught up in the worship as well.

After the worship part, it was offering time. I made sure I set aside a nice offering for the church and for Prophet Lincoln. A workman was worthy of his meat.

Once the offering was complete, it was Prophet Lincoln's time to preach.

"Praise the Lord, everybody!" he screamed into the microphone.

A few people shouted with him.

"Come on, you can do better than that. Who came for a revival?"

More people shouted, and I raised my voice even louder with the congregation.

"The Lord told me somebody needed a word tonight! There is a word in the building, yessuh!"

My heart flip-flopped. This was it.

"I'm not even gonna preach no sermon tonight. The Lord told me that it's time to prophesy. You hear me, church? I said, it's time to prophesy!"

The organist and the rest of the musicians caught on to Prophet Lincoln's direction. They played in tune with his voice until there was complete harmony.

"Anybody need a word from the Lord?" Prophet Lincoln drew out his words as he hollered.

Hands shot up all around the room, and one of the musicians created a buildup sound with the cymbals.

"The Lord has a word for you today!" Prophet Lincoln thundered.

Gasps could be heard as he leapt on top of one of the pews, landing in front of Sister Dorsey. She almost fell back from the suddenness of Bishop's movement.

We watched as he prophesied to her. "The Lord said he's gonna do it, my sister! He's gonna give you that job!" Sister Dorsey began shouting, and others clapped and shouted with her. Prophet Lincoln hopped over that pew and landed on another pew in front of Brother Green. Brother Green made a face at him like he wasn't pleased.

Prophet Lincoln pointed at him. "The Lord said you're waiting on a promotion. It's coming! It's coming, my brother! Before you know it, it will be here!"

The congregation continued to shout as Brother Green gave a soft hand clap, but not much more. I didn't understand why Brother Green didn't seem to be happy. Who wouldn't want a promotion?

I watched as Prophet Lincoln continued to hop pews on one side of the church, then finally, he took a few steps back and leapt clean across the aisle to start on our side.

I knew he was coming for me soon.

Chapter 8

Nicole

I prayed with all my might that the crazy man would stay over on the other side of the church, but he jumped across the aisle to our side.

I could not believe Zakari's pastor was allowing this.

The man had no respect for God's church. He was jumping on pews like he bought them. I was always taught that the sanctuary was a place of reverence, but this man was treating it like some kind of circus. He was jumping the pews then leaning down to scream in people's faces.

I was terrified.

My eyes shot from left to right to see if anyone agreed with me that this man was out of order. Zakari was standing next to me on my left side. He was clapping and shouting along with most of the other members of his church, so I was sure he wouldn't want to leave. I looked to my right, and one of the sisters from Zakari's church was standing on that side, and she was shouting and waving at Prophet Lincoln as well.

I had to escape.

Something told me that Prophet Lincoln was going to come to our row soon, and I wanted no parts of it.

One of the brothers he prophesied to on the other side of the church looked upset at him. I glanced over to observe him, and his fists were balled at his sides.

Finally, somebody who disagreed with what was happening tonight.

I was so busy looking at the brother who was upset that I didn't notice Prophet Lincoln's loud voice was getting closer.

He jumped another pew and almost landed on top of the person he was prophesying to next.

The woman looked frightened, and rightfully so. Prophet Lincoln laid a hand on her head and screamed in her ear but held the microphone in his other hand so his words could be heard by the rest of us. "The Lord said to tell you not to worry, my sister! Everything is gonna be alright!"

I watched with trepidation as Prophet Lincoln's ushers ran after him from row to row as he continued to hop pews. I wanted to walk out of the church, but I was afraid.

What if he caught me on the way out? I didn't want him screaming in my face like he did with those other people.

We had people prophesy at our church before, but it was nothing like this. The preacher didn't jump on top of pews and yell at people. He spoke calmly, and the things he said were very specific. He also didn't go to multiple people in the church like it was some kind of spectacle. I didn't know everything about church, God, or the Bible, but something about this wasn't right.

My heart dropped as Prophet Lincoln hopped over one row, then another, and stopped short in front of Zakari.

"Oh Lord," I prayed under my breath. "Please, no."

Zakari looked over at me in excitement, then back up at Prophet Lincoln.

I braced myself for whatever Prophet Lincoln was about to say.

Chapter 9

Zakari

I could hardly keep still as Prophet Lincoln stopped in front of me.

"Young man?" he said.

"Yes, sir?" I stood up straighter.

He looked between me and Nicole. "This your girlfriend?"

I looked at Nicole, then back at Prophet Lincoln.

"Yes, sir."

"The Lord told me to tell you, she's gonna be your wife!"

My jaw dropped, and Nicole gasped beside me as thunderous applause broke out around us. Prophet Lincoln went to another pew after that, but I couldn't get his words out of my mind. I couldn't believe it. Nicole was going to be my wife?

How did he know that was what I was praying about?

How did he know Nicole was my girlfriend?

The Lord sure worked in mysterious ways.

I looked over at Nicole to see if she was feeling what I was feeling. She was focused on the pew behind us, where Prophet Lincoln was prophesying to someone else. "The Lord told me to tell you, you're last, but not least! My brother, the last shall be first, and the first shall be last!" The man fell out from the prayer, and Prophet Lincoln's ushers fanned him. After that, Prophet Lincoln got down from the pew he was standing on and strode to the front of the church, humming along with the music the musicians were playing along the way. "Hmm, yes Lord," he kept saying until he got to the front.

When he arrived at the front, he said, "Saints, the Lord has impressed something else upon my heart. He said... ooh, Lord! He said the word *sacrifice*. Sometimes the Lord calls us to sacrifice and to sow a seed, so we can reap a harvest."

A solemn expression grew on Prophet Lincoln's face as the music lowered in sound with his tone. "Yes, yes... There are fifty people in this room that the Lord said he wants to sow a seed. You're in need of a blessing, yessuh. Fifty people. Fifty people need to give fifty dollars. The Lord said to test him on this. If you give fifty dollars as a sacrificial seed on tonight, the Lord will expedite your blessing! Yes, Lord!"

The first person shot out of their row and ran to place the money at the prophet's feet. He continued to stand as other people got up and went to give their sacrificial seeds as well.

I wanted to go but wasn't sure if I should. I wanted the Lord to expedite my blessing, too, but was I one of the fifty?"

As if he heard my thoughts, Prophet Lincoln spoke again.

"The Lord said don't question it, just do it!"

That was all I needed. I hurried and brought the last of my allowance to the front of the church and laid it at Prophet Lincoln's feet. The area in front of him was covered in bills. The Lord was surely moving on tonight.

I went back to my seat with renewed conviction. God had already spoken on my behalf. All I had to do was sit tight and wait for everything to work in my favor.

Chapter 10

Nicole

My mind was spinning when I got home. Thankfully, Zakari didn't mention Prophet Lincoln's prophecy as he dropped me off, but I could tell from his facial expression when the man was saying it that Zakari believed his words.

Did this mean I had to marry him now?

How could a person know if a prophecy was real?

I was confused. It wasn't like Zakari was a bad guy... Maybe Prophet Lincoln saw something I didn't. Maybe I was being too harsh. Shareese often said I was judgmental, and I tried not to be, but sometimes I felt certain things were uncalled for. Was I being too harsh?

No one else at Zakari's church except that one brother with his fists balled up seemed to have a problem with Prophet Lincoln's style. Fifty people had even gone up after he finished prophesying to sow a sacrificial seed. That was twenty-five hundred dollars! It couldn't have been wrong. Zakari's pastor didn't say anything negative after Prophet Lincoln finished. He just got up and said the Bishop gave a good word, and they would be returning the next night for more preaching.

I didn't know what to make of it.

I went to my mom's room to ask her, but as I approached her door, I heard her on the phone having a heated discussion with my father. I knew it was him based on her tone of voice and the things she was saying.

"This is the third time, Nathaniel!" she shouted.

Yup, she was talking to my dad.

I didn't even want to know what that was about. My mom never told me what she and my dad argued about. Even when they got divorced. She just said they weren't able to get along, and they both loved me, but they didn't love each other the same way.

For some reason, that memory caused me to burst into tears.

I went back to my bedroom and closed the door.

My mom called me down for dinner a few hours later. She was much calmer than she had been earlier, so I didn't bring up the fact that I heard her and my father arguing.

"When is your last day of work this summer?" she asked.

I finished my bite of broccoli. "August twenty sixth."

"Good." She nodded. "Your father wants us all to go out to dinner for your last official night here. We're so proud of you, Nicole."

A tear came to her eyes, but I knew she was about to cry for a different reason than the fact that she was proud of me. I suspected it had something to do with whatever they were arguing about.

A thought dawned on me. "Mom, are you going to be okay with me gone?"

She paused when I asked that. "What do you mean?"

"I mean, because... you know... Dad is gone, and now I'm leaving. I don't want you to be lonely."

My mother stared at me for a long time before speaking again.

"Nicole, don't you worry about me. You go on to school and have fun. Take your classes seriously, don't get stuck on any relationships, and join every club or activity that interests you. This is your time to explore."

My mind zeroed in on the part where she said not to get stuck on any relationships. Was she talking about me and Zakari?

I wanted to ask, but then I didn't.

We finished our meal and chatted about other things. By the end of the night, I was back to being excited about my future.

Chapter 11

Zakari

If Nicole and I were going to be married, I wanted to at least get her a promise ring before we went to college.

There wasn't much time left, seeing that the end of August was swiftly approaching. It had been a few weeks since Prophet Lincoln's revival at my church, but his words stuck with me. He said it plain as day, Nicole was my wife.

I looked online for a few rings, but none of the ones I saw would do Nicole justice. I went out to the mall instead and opened up a credit line with one of the jewelry stores. The salesman tried to get me to lock down on a decision, but this was serious. I wasn't picking a ring until I knew it was perfect.

I envisioned myself and Nicole on our wedding day. She would walk down the aisle in her pretty white dress, and I would stand at the front with Pastor in my black suit and necktie. I would be looking sharp. My friend, Lester, would probably be my best man, and Shareese would be Nicole's maid of honor. Maybe some of the sisters from her church could be bridesmaids? And brothers from my church could be groomsmen? I went on my phone as I sat in the food court to look up how many people were supposed to be in a wedding party. Then that got me to thinking, who would be our ring bearer?

Sister Michaels just had a baby. Maybe once Nicole and I graduated college and got married, her and Brother Michaels would agree for us to let their son walk our rings down the aisle. He was so cute.

My mind went to me and Nicole's future children next. What would they look like? I imagined the boys would look like me, and the girls like Nicole. How many children would we have? I was thinking we could stop after maybe six. Three boys and three girls, if the Lord worked it out that way. Regardless of how it turned out, I would love all our children the same.

All that thinking of Nicole must have conjured her up, because there she was, walking past me to one of the restaurants at the food court. She was carrying two large plastic bags from different clothing stores. I thought she said she was working until ten tonight? Her boss must have let her off early.

"Hey!" I called out to get her attention. When she turned, I waved.

Nicole gave me a smile and approached. "What are you doing here?"

"I was going to ask you the same thing. Weren't you supposed to work tonight?"

Nicole paused like she didn't remember telling me that. "Right, I was, but I called out."

"Ooh, look at you playing hooky," I teased.

Nicole didn't respond.

"Wanna sit down?" I gestured.

"Sure." She pulled back the chair across from me, then stopped. "Actually, I was going to grab something to eat."

"That's fine! We can eat together. Or you can since I'm already done."

More silence, then she said, "Okay. I'll be right back."

I watched as Nicole walked toward one of the fast-food spots to place her order. Was something wrong? She didn't seem too enthusiastic about sitting down to eat with me. Maybe she was upset about something. She did say she called out of work.

When Nicole returned with her food tray, I was ready to set her at ease.

"How's your day going?"

I watched as she took a bite of her sandwich before responding.

"It was good, how was yours?"

"It's great! I actually..." I stopped myself. I didn't want to let her in on the surprise. Should it be a surprise? Maybe it shouldn't be. Maybe that was why I couldn't find the perfect promise ring because Nicole needed to pick it out herself!

"You actually what?" Nicole stared at me with intrigue.

I swallowed. "I was going to say I came here for a specific reason today."

She looked around me as if trying to find something, then said, "What did you come for? I don't see any bags."

I could hardly mask my excitement. "That's the thing. I tried to do it myself, but I should have had you come with me."

Nicole wrinkled her nose. "Zakari, what are you talking about?"

"I was going to get you a promise ring. I figured we are too young for engagement, but a promise ring will hold us over until we're ready."

Nicole fell silent, then sat back. "Zakari, I need to tell you something."

My heart dropped. It didn't look like whatever she was about to tell me was good.

"What is it, Nicole? Is everything okay? Did something happen?"

She shook her head. "No, nothing happened. It's about our relationship, though." She looked down then back up at me with questions in her eyes like she was asking for my permission to continue. I nodded.

"I think we should break things off."

It was my turn to get tongue-tied. "Break things off?" I repeated.

She nodded. "I don't want to be in a relationship while I'm in college. We're too young."

"Too young?"

She nodded, and I didn't understand, but I tried to.

Nicole reached out and grabbed my hand. "Maybe we can pick back up again once we graduate, but if you happen to find someone else at your school, I won't get upset."

I didn't know what to say.

"Okay," I mustered, and Nicole's face broke out in a big smile.

Chapter 12

Nicole

As soon as Zakari agreed with me, a huge weight fell off my shoulders.
 I felt good. Free. I could relax and focus on my future now. Zakari and I would keep in touch. We were still friends, after all, but I was sure he would find someone new at his school, and so would I.

Either way, now wasn't the time to worry about that. It was time to celebrate.

The last few weeks of the summer flew by, and before I knew it, it was time to go.

Shareese called me over to her house the day before I caught my flight across the country. We were going to spend the night together then go our separate ways.

On my way to her house, I called Zakari to see how he was doing. We hadn't spoken much since I broke things off with him.

"Hello?" he answered on the first ring. He sounded testy, so I wasn't sure if this was a good time. Still, I kept a lighthearted tone as I greeted him.

"Hey, Zakari! How are you?"

"I'm good. How are you?"

"Good. Excited to head off to school. Did you leave already?"

"No, I didn't leave yet."

"Oh, well, I'm leaving tomorrow. I hope you have a safe trip whenever you do go. Oh, and let's keep in touch.

We don't have to be strangers just because we're going to different schools."

"Really? You want to keep in touch?" His tone considerably lightened.

I giggled. "Of course, silly. We got history, boy!"

Zakari giggled, too. "Right, we sure do. Safe travels, Nicole, and let me know when you touch down."

"I sure will! Have a good night."

"You too!"

I hung up with a smile. I had heard so many stories about bad breakups, but me and Zakari were nothing like that. We would keep our friendship despite going our separate ways.

"Thank you, Lord," I said as the Uber driver pulled up to Shareese's house. She was standing on the porch waiting for me.

"Hey!" I bounced up the stairs to give her a hug.

"Hey, bestie!" She wore an expression of excitement.

"What's going on with you?" I asked, catching on, though not knowing what it was.

"I have been holding back a secret from you, but it's time to tell."

"What is it?" I braced myself, knowing whatever it was, it was good.

"I got a letter a few weeks ago from Rockland."

My heart leapt. "What? You did? What did they say?" I already knew the answer based on her excitement, and I was ready to jump with joy, but I wanted Shareese to say it.

"They reconsidered my admission, and I got in!"

"Yes!" We screamed in unison and hugged each other again. When we pulled back, there were tears in both of our eyes.

"I can't believe it! We're going to Rockland together!" I wiped a tear from my cheek.

"Me either. It's like a dream come true," Shareese said, wiping her eyes as well.

Zakari and I were remaining friends, and Shareese was coming to Rockland? This day could not get any better.

Chapter 13

Zakari

I had no idea what I was going to do with myself until I got that phone call from Nicole. Silly me. I thought we were breaking up for good when we talked at the mall.

My mom did always say I had trouble reading people.

I chuckled as I thought of the day I had when she spilled the beans about wanting to break things off.

Now that I thought of it, I was being a little dramatic by stabbing a hole through my jewelry store credit card with a butcher knife. Not to mention, damaging my desk in the process. Silly me. Now I would have to go and get a new card. Good thing I didn't close the account altogether.

My last day of work was today, then I was going to head to my college like Nicole did the other day.

I got the surprise of my life when I saw the selfie her and Shareese posted in front of their new school. "Oh, wow, I thought Shareese didn't get accepted to Rockland." Then I read the comments and understood. The school appealed her application. I didn't know they could do that sort of thing. Maybe I should have tried it.

Too late now, but it didn't matter, anyway. Me and Nicole's relationship was fine. We were just taking a break for college.

We would keep up with each other until we graduated, then it would be on.

My phone buzzed with a text from Lester. I chuckled again, thinking of my dramatics due to the little misunderstanding I had with Nicole.

I had been ignoring Lester's calls and texts, but now it was time to answer him. I called his phone.

"Hey, bro," he answered. "What's been good with you?"

"Nothing, just getting ready to head off to school. You ready?" Lester was going to Wayson College like me. We were going to have a blast, I knew it.

"Absolutely. I can't wait to see what the ladies are looking like."

I chuckled. Lester was such a player.

More power to him, but I was a one-woman man. I had already found my forever in Nicole. Lester never seemed to understand our relationship, but one day he would when he found a woman of his own.

"What time are we leaving in the morning again?" Lester asked. He was riding with me in my car, then my parents were driving their car. Lester's parents weren't coming.

"We're leaving at six on the dot. Don't have us waiting, either, or we'll leave you, man," I joked. I would never leave Lester behind.

Lester and his parents didn't have the same type of relationship my parents had with me. Lester didn't seem too upset about it, though. He often bragged that he would be glad to get away from them.

My parents were cool, so I didn't mind them around. They gave me my space to be a man, so I wasn't pressed for freedom like other teens.

I wondered what Nicole was doing.

I checked her page earlier today, but I needed to check it again to see what her and Shareese were up to.

They were probably having a blast at orientation like me and Lester would be in a few short hours.

"Zakari?" Lester was saying. I almost forgot he was on the phone since I was so focused on Nicole's page. No updates.

"Yeah?" I answered.

"I was saying I'll see you in the morning."

"Okay cool. See you."

We hung up, and I stared at the blown-up selfie of me and Nicole on my wall before falling fast asleep.

Chapter 14

Zakari

Why hadn't Nicole posted any updates? I had been checking her page for the past two days and hadn't seen anything. Lester and I were on our way to Wayson, so I could only scroll social media at rest stops, but still... What was going on? Did something happen?

Maybe I should just call her. I chuckled and relaxed when I realized that was what I should have been doing all along.

Lester glanced at me from the highway. He was driving since we switched spots at the last rest stop. We were over the halfway point in our travels, and my parents were keeping up pretty good.

"What's wrong with you?" he asked.

I was already dialing Nicole's number, so I didn't answer him, but she didn't pick up. Probably still in orientation. I would try back later once we arrived at our school.

The moment Lester parked at the freshman dormitory we would be staying at, I called Nicole again. I relaxed when she answered.

"Hello?" I heard other voices in the background. Probably her dormmates.

"Hello, missy! How are things?"

"They're good, Zakari. How are things with you? Did you leave for your school yet?"

I smiled and glanced over at Lester, who looked like he was getting impatient. "We sure did. Lester is here with me, like Shareese is there with you."

Nicole didn't answer, but I still heard voices in the background, so I figured someone was distracting her.

"Nicole?"

"Huh? Oh yeah. Let me call you back, Zakari. I am about to head into this meeting."

She hung up before I could ask her what the meeting was about.

I chuckled and looked at Lester. "Busy woman." I rolled my eyes playfully.

Lester stared at me like something was wrong. "I thought you and Nicole broke up?"

"Huh?" I was confused for a second, then I remembered I hadn't updated him on our status. "Oh yeah, we're back together."

His forehead creased. "You are?"

I nodded. "Yup, we're just taking a break for college, then we'll get back together."

Lester stopped mid-movement as he was unclicking his seatbelt. "So, you're not back together then."

"Yes, we are. We're just waiting 'til we graduate to get married."

"Zakari..."

"What?"

"What was the exact conversation you and Nicole had when you believed y'all got back together?"

I felt my ears grow hot. "What do you mean, what was the exact conversation? You think I don't know my own girlfriend? What's your problem, man?"

Lester unclicked his seatbelt, then held his hands up. "Look, Zakari, I'm not trying to start an argument, but you know you have a problem reading people sometimes."

"Yes, I do, but Nicole gave me clarification when we talked. I'm not stupid, Lester. I'm going to give her space while we're in college, then we're getting back together."

"And what if she finds another guy while she's out there?"

I opened my mouth to tell him she wouldn't do that to me, but my parents were standing outside our car. They must have just pulled in the parking lot.

"We gotta get moving," I said instead.

Lester didn't respond, so I got out of the car, and he followed suit. We didn't say much else to each other as we brought all our stuff up to our room. I was glad I had my best friend as my roommate rather than anyone else.

I was sure the other guys at this school would be cool, too, but there was nothing like living with someone you already knew.

When my parents left, Lester tried to bring up Nicole again, but I changed the subject. He was being a hater about our relationship, truth be told. I tried not to call him on it, but sooner or later, I would have to.

I knew what Prophet Lincoln said. The prophecy was clear. All I had to do was wait out these four years, just like Jacob waited fourteen years for Rachel. If he could wait that long, I certainly could do so for a shorter time frame.

Sooner or later, Lester would see.

Chapter 15

Zakari

Nicole hadn't been answering her phone calls for the past few days.

I understood she was busy because she just moved in, but I was busy too and still made time for her. What was going on?

I wouldn't dare ask Lester because he would start hating again. Lester was such a dog. He was already making moves on two different girls, one of the Resident Advisors from our dorm and another girl in a different dorm. Both were upperclassmen.

I wasn't going to snitch on him, though, because unlike him, I wasn't a hater. I gave him his space to do what he wanted. I didn't understand why he wouldn't do the same for me.

Lester wasn't all bad, though. We had a great time when he wasn't trying to sabotage what I had with Nicole.

Speaking of Nicole, she was calling me.

"See?" I said to no one since Lester was in Maria's room. "Hello?"

"Hey, Zakari!" Nicole sounded breathless, and it turned me on. I wished she was here at my school so I could grab her up and kiss her. Her lips were so soft, like pillows. I couldn't wait for my lips to connect with them again.

"Hey yourself," I joked. "I see you've been busy."

"Yeah, sorry about that. This whole week has been a whirlwind, but we started classes the other day, and they are going good."

I relaxed. That must have been the meeting she was referring to the other day. A class meeting, duh.

"What are you taking this semester?" I asked.

"Mostly general education requirements. Biology, Algebra, Spanish, then I have one business class."

I smiled. "That's great! I start my classes tomorrow, but they put me in everything related to my major. Mechanical Engineering sounds like it's going to be a challenge."

"It probably will be, but I'm sure it's nothing you can't handle, Zakari. You've always been really smart in math and science."

My heart fluttered. "Thanks, babe."

She fell silent.

"Nicole?"

"Hey, Zakari, I've gotta go. Me and Shareese are headed to a party."

"Ooh, don't do anything I wouldn't do!" I laughed.

"I won't. We'll catch up later."

She hung up before I could say anything else, but I didn't mind. Nicole and Shareese were about to have a blast at their party, which made me decide to go ahead and take Lester up on his offer to go to a party tonight at our school.

I went to my closet to put together a fly outfit.

I was about to show these Wayson guys how it was done. I might have been a nerd due to my interests in math and science, but I always knew how to dress.

I threw a few things together and was about to hop in the shower when Lester walked in our room. He stared at the outfit on my bed.

"Good, you're going!"

"Of course, I am. Can't leave you out there hanging, bro!"

I dapped him up, then went to take my shower.

Seven years later...

Chapter 16

Nicole

Jerron and I walked hand in hand through the mall.

I swore, this man was like a dream come true. I could not believe how he swooped into my life and took my breath away. We met in college and dated off and on throughout the years, but it wasn't anything serious.

When the time came to graduate, he didn't want to let me go. I didn't admit it at the time, but I didn't want to let him go, either.

We decided to take our relationship seriously as we pursued our master's degrees at different schools. It was tough, being that we were long distance, but we managed. On the day of my graduation, Jerron surprised me in front of my whole family by getting down on bended knee and proposing. The moment was magical, and the ring was beautiful. I saw nothing but love and desire in his eyes, and my features expressed the same emotion.

That was why I couldn't understand how we still weren't married a whole year later.

We thought of a few dates in the beginning when the excitement was high, but Jerron kept pushing the dates back. I wondered why.

Was he getting cold feet?
Did he no longer love me?
Was it because I hadn't given him my virginity?

All those things could be true. There were times when Jerron seemed distant, but then again, I wasn't sure. Maybe I was reading too much into things. When I brought up our wedding date, and even mentioned that my family was asking about it, he would change the subject. What was going on? I wanted to ask him now, but we were at the mall, so I continued walking with him, hand in hand, as we went shopping for something to wear to Mike and Tina's Jack and Jill.

Yup, our friends from college, who had gotten engaged after us, were getting married before us. I would have thought when Mike proposed to Tina, Jerron would have stepped his game up to compete with his best friend, but he didn't.

I was happy for my girl, Tina, though, despite me and Jerron's issues. I met her through Jerron and Mike, of course. Mike and Tina started dating after college, then things grew serious when she got pregnant. He proposed within a few weeks of finding out the news. That was why I wondered what was going on with Jerron. Was he mad at me because I didn't give myself to him like Tina did with Mike?

We had come close more than a few times, but I never gave in. I set boundaries to help us stay on track and not give into temptation.

Maybe Jerron didn't agree with the boundaries.

Maybe he wished I had gone all the way with him.

I glanced down at our hands. We were walking together as if we were united, but were we really? The only one who could answer that question was Jerron.

I opened my mouth to say something, but he stopped short.

I looked up at him, wondering what was going on and watched as his jaw dropped.

"Shameka? Oh wow!"

Shameka? My eyes shot to the woman he was ogling over. I dropped Jerron's hand, but he didn't seem to notice. I assessed her with my eyes, and she didn't seem to notice I was doing so because she was just as caught up in Jerron as he was in her.

"Jerron, OMG!" She jumped and hugged him, and he hugged her back.

Okay, they were doing too much for me.

"Hello," I said, cutting into their little reunion.

Shameka seemed to notice me for the first time. "Hi." She pulled back from Jerron, giving me a strange look like she wondered who I was.

Jerron clapped his hand over his mouth. "Oh, my bad. Shameka, this is Nicole. Nicole, this is Shameka. Shameka was my high school sweetheart."

I was taken aback by all this information. Shameka was his high school sweetheart? How come I never heard of her? And more importantly, why was he introducing her to me, and not me to her? Why didn't he mention that I was his fiancée?

Outwardly, I put on a friendly smile and stood there while they exchanged pleasantries, but on the inside, I was stewing. Jerron was certainly getting a piece of my mind as soon as we were alone.

At the end of their five minute interaction, they had the nerve to exchange numbers.

Like I wasn't even there.

That part hurt, but I pretended not to let it affect me.

When Miss Shameka finally walked away, Jerron stared after her for a few moments, still with that stupid look on his face before he remembered I was standing here.

"Wow, Nicole, that was like walking down memory lane. I haven't seen Shameka in years."

I had heard enough about Shameka within the last five minutes to last a lifetime, but I still wasn't ready to show it.

"I gathered," I said instead.

Jerron's brows furrowed. "What's wrong with you?"

"Nothing." I walked into one of the clothing stores to find an outfit.

Chapter 17

Nicole

Jerron followed me into the second store, hot on my heels. I had completely ignored him in the first store I walked into. "Nicole. Nicole!" He gently grabbed my arm, and I could no longer help it. I turned around to face him with tears in my eyes.

He was perplexed. "Nicole, what's going on?"

I sniffled. "What was that back there, Jerron?"

"What was what back where?" His cluelessness was pissing me off.

"That woman. You didn't even tell her I was your fiancée, then this is the first time I'm hearing about a high school sweetheart? What is going on, Jerron?"

"Huh? Nicole, that wasn't anything to be worried about. Shameka and I dated in high school. Maybe I shouldn't have said she was my sweetheart. We were together, but it was more sexual than anything..." He stopped himself before continuing as if he'd said too much. That bit he shared caused all types of alarm bells and questions in my mind. It was all sexual? Did she take his virginity? Why did he get her number?

I asked my last question first. "Why did you exchange numbers with her like I wasn't even standing there? Do you realize how disrespectful that was?"

Jerron looked taken aback. "Disrespectful? How so?"

"You just told me that you had a sexual relationship with this woman."

"Almost ten years ago."

Now he was trying to make me look stupid. I didn't like it. "Delete her number, Jerron." I crossed my arms over my chest.

He gave me a confused stare. "Nicole, I don't understand why you are so upset. Me and Shameka have nothing going on. I literally just saw her out of nowhere. She's nothing more than an old friend."

"An old friend you had sex with!"

Finally, he seemed to get it. He visibly relaxed. "Okay, I gotchu." He pulled out his phone, and I watched as he deleted Shameka's number. "We good?" he asked.

Part of my tension eased as well. "We're better than we were a minute ago, but we still need to talk."

"About what? What did I do now?"

Jerron was starting to irritate me with this act he was putting on. How could he not know why I was upset? He was just head over heels for that Shameka woman, who he claimed he left almost a decade ago, and here I was with an engagement ring but no wedding date.

I resumed walking through the aisles looking for cute dresses to take my mind off my problems. Jerron pestered me for a few moments, asking questions about why I was still upset, but I ignored him. If he couldn't figure it out, I wasn't going to help him.

I settled on an outfit, and we went to another store that featured men's clothing so he could do the same.

After that, we shared an awkward meal in the food court. Shameka walked by us and waved, and he got googly eyed and waved back.

That was it for me. I didn't finish the rest of my meal.

Chapter 18

Nicole

On the ride home, Jerron tried to engage with me again.

"Are you ready to tell me what's upsetting you?"

It was time to let him have it. I turned in my seat to face him, which was somewhat difficult seeing that I was wearing a seatbelt, but he would know from my gesture I was serious. "Jerron, when are we getting married?"

Silence.

Just as I suspected.

He continued to drive as if he hadn't heard my question. I wasn't backing down this time. "Did you hear me?"

He sighed and turned down a side street. "Yes, Nicole."

The tears tried to creep back up. "Why won't you answer me then? We've been engaged over a year and have yet to set a date, Jerron. Don't you see anything wrong with that?"

He pulled over and unclicked his seatbelt, then turned to face me. "Nicole, I'm sorry."

That threw me for a loop.

He was apologizing? For what? For putting off the date or something else? Was it someone else? Maybe Shameka wasn't the only woman I needed to be worried about.

"What are you sorry for?" I prodded, since he left his sentence open as if he wanted me to persuade him to continue.

"For putting off the date. I guess I got scared."

Alarm bells rang again. "Scared how? Like you don't want to get married?" I unclicked my seatbelt, too. I didn't know what I would do if Jerron said he didn't want to get married.

He shook his head. "No, nothing like that. I definitely want to get married."

My shoulders un-tensed.

"It's just..." he continued, then stopped.

"Spit it out."

"Don't you think we should be more established? I mean, we both have our master's degrees, and you found a great job, but I still haven't found anything. I had my heart set on working at my internship site, but you see how that fell through. I feel like I have nothing to offer you."

He looked away when he said that, as if he'd just confessed his deepest fear, and it broke my heart.

"Jerron!" I grabbed his hand, the tears returning to my eyes.

He turned to face me again.

"Listen, you will find your dream job. You just have to have faith. That internship position didn't go through, but maybe that was for a reason. Think about it. Your school was six hours away, and we always wanted to go back to our home state to settle down. If you would have gotten that job, you would have had to stay away."

Jerron had grown up in Connecticut like I did, but he was from a different city, so we never met until we entered college at Rockland.

Jerron's features softened as if I said something he hadn't considered. "True. But I've been applying to places like crazy, and they keep saying they want all this experience like my internship didn't count. Then I had those three botched interviews, back-to-back. It seems like as soon as I have hope, it gets snatched away."

I intertwined my fingers with his.

"Jerron, that's nothing to worry about. You will find a job. I know it's tough with the economy, but I have full faith you will find something. God did not bring you this far just to leave you here."

He nodded like a weight was lifted from his chest.

"Let's pray," I continued. "Father God, we come before you asking that you help Jerron get a job. Lord, you saw his hard work and dedication while he was in college and grad school, and even on his internship. Lord, you open doors that no man can shut and shut doors no man can open. We pray you intercede on his behalf. In Jesus' name, Amen."

When I opened my eyes from the prayer, Jerron was staring at me with googly eyes that were way more intense than the ones he had for that Shameka woman.

At that moment, I felt a confirmation in my heart. It shocked me because it wasn't often I felt such a thing. I focused back on Jerron. He was still giving me that look, but his expression changed when he saw that mine did.

"What is it?" he asked.

"Didn't you say you had another interview coming up tomorrow?"

He nodded. "Yes, but..."

"You're going to get it," I cut him off.

He looked surprised. "Huh? How do you..."

"The Lord just told me you're going to get it."

Jerron contemplated it for a moment. "Nicole, if I get that job, we can get married before summer."

It was March, so that was barely three months away.

I chuckled. "Alright now, don't be writing checks you can't cash, because you're getting that job tomorrow."

"Okay, Miss Prophet. We'll see."

Chapter 19

Nicole

The next day, I went to work at Noble Hospital. I was a quality improvement manager, which meant I was loved by my superiors but often hated by those I had to oversee. Some of the lower-level managers couldn't seem to understand the hospital had protocols in place for a reason. I understood patient loads were heavy and that anything in healthcare was a difficult job, but we had the task of helping people heal and keeping them safe. We couldn't do that if our systems had holes in them or if we cut corners while providing their care.

Despite the serious nature of my position, I was fair to the people I was assigned to oversee. I always gave second chances and provided trainings and tips to help make the process smoother. Some of my employees listened while others didn't.

Thankfully, today was a breeze.

I checked my phone every so often for a call or text from Jerron. His interview was at noon, so he should have reached out to me by one or two.

When five o'clock rolled around and I still hadn't heard from him, I got worried.

Did he not get the job?

I was sure the Lord confirmed with me that he would.

Why hadn't he called or texted me?

I called him on my Bluetooth on the way to my apartment, but it went straight to voicemail. Something was wrong.

I made a U-turn and headed toward his place. He was staying with Mike for the time being but was soon to be kicked out when Mike and Tina got married.

I drove up his street and saw that his car was parked outside, along with Mike's and Tina's. This was strange.

He was sitting here at home but turned his phone off? What was going on?

I walked up to the door and knocked.

"Come on in!" Mike yelled from the inside.

I opened the door and jumped as Mike, Tina, and Jerron screamed in unison. "Surprise!"

I stared at their silly kiddie party hats and watched as Tina blew on one of those little party favor things that made a horn sound.

"What in the world...?"

Jerron stepped toward me, beaming. "I guess I'm a prophet, too. The Lord showed me you would come here looking for me."

His eyes twinkled, and I giggled. "Jerron, what is going on?"

"I got the job, babe! And Mike and Tina wanted to throw something together to re-celebrate our engagement. How does June first sound as a wedding date?"

My jaw dropped. I didn't know what question to ask first, so I asked them all.

"You got the job? We're getting married? Is this real?"

"Yes to all three." Jerron wrapped me up in a hug, then sealed it with a kiss. When we pulled back, he stared in my eyes, his love and devotion shining through.

"We're getting married, baby. No more delays."

Chapter 20

Nicole

I was bursting with excitement after Jerron made his announcement.

We had a wedding to plan. All this time I had been waiting on a date, and now it was moving toward me like a freight train.

I needed a dress, a venue, caterers... Oh, Lord, my brain was starting to hurt. How on earth were we going to pull this off in three months?

I needed to call my pastor. No, I needed to call my mother and father first. No, Shareese.

Good Lord, my mind was all over the place.

I called Shareese. "Hey, girl," she answered. She sounded depressed, which knocked me right out of my good mood.

"Hey, Shareese, what's going on?"

"I was just about to call you. I'm not sure if it means anything, but I felt you should know."

I stared at my living room wall. This didn't sound like good news, whatever it was. "What is it, Shareese?"

"Nicole, I'm going to send you a picture. You tell me if this is anything to be concerned about."

What picture? What was she sending me?

I waited until the picture Shareese sent me loaded into our text thread. When I saw it, my body grew hot and cold.

I could not believe what I was seeing.

No, he did not.

The day after he proposed?

How could he?

I couldn't be seeing what I was seeing.

It simply wasn't true. That wasn't Jerron.

Sitting at a coffee shop across from Shameka. Smiling. Looking like they were sharing a joke, probably about me.

"Let me call you back," I said to Shareese, then hung up before she had a chance to say anything back to me.

I called Jerron, but it went to voicemail.

That infuriated me. How dare he? How could he? He told me she was an old friend from a long time ago. I couldn't believe I believed him.

My thoughts swirled for a moment, then the more rational side of my mind started to kick in.

Maybe it was innocent.

How could it be, though, when we just had a conversation about this woman the other day? I knew I was clear with my words when I demanded Jerron delete her number from his phone. He did it right in front of me, and now he was having coffee with her?

This wasn't happening.

I called Shareese back.

"Hello?" she answered.

"When was that picture taken?" I boomed as if she was the one in the wrong.

"This morning. I just saw them, and I bugged out at first, but then I remembered you were complaining about how Jerron kept putting off y'all wedding date, and I was wondering if this was why."

I almost opened my mouth to tell her what happened the day prior, how Jerron got offered the job and we finally had a date, but I couldn't.

Just that quickly, my hope was snatched from under my feet.

"Shareese, let me call you back," I repeated and hung up again.

I called Jerron, and it rang, but he didn't answer.

My heart sank.

I just lost the love of my life.

Chapter 21

Zakari

Nicole changed her status to Engaged.

What did she mean, engaged? I hadn't proposed to her yet. I clicked on her profile and didn't see any pictures. Then I clicked on the notification itself, and it wouldn't tell me who she was engaged to. What was going on?

I called her phone, but she didn't answer.

Why wasn't she answering?

This wasn't like Nicole... well, actually it was, but usually only when she was busy. Nicole and I had kept frequent contact all through college and grad school. She dated a few guys off and on, but she always assured me it was never serious. I dated a few people, too. But then we lost touch last year, or maybe the year before. I couldn't remember. I had been meaning to reach back out to her, but things at work were picking up heavily. I was a mechanical engineer for a growing enterprise. We were expanding all over the city, and there were further opportunities down the pipeline to go nationwide. It was an exciting time for me, but I hadn't had a chance to update Nicole.

I kicked myself for that. I didn't even get to show her the house I built for us yet.

Well, I didn't build it myself, but I had it built for us.

It was perfect, she would see.

But what was she talking about... she was engaged? I racked my brains to think of the last guy she said she was dating. Jerron was his name. I checked out his pictures, but he was no match for me. Whatever he and Nicole shared couldn't hold a candle to the flames of passion between me and my woman.

I needed to get in contact with Nicole and soon.

"Maybe she was just joking," I said to myself. "Yeah, that's what it is." I relaxed. Nicole wouldn't do that to me. She wouldn't string me along for seven years, the same time Jacob waited for Rachel, just to let me down.

Well, Jacob ended up working for fourteen years in total, but that was in Bible times. I worked hard to make sure everything was perfect for us. Nicole was going to love our house. It had eight bedrooms, a full-blown mansion. Maybe not a mansion, but still nice and big enough for all our future children. On top of owning the house, we also had three acres of land. Nicole was going to be so excited. I couldn't wait to show her.

She would have everything she wanted. She didn't even have to work if she didn't want to. I was prepared to pick back up where we left off in high school, just like she promised.

I checked her page once again.

I was scrolling through her Congratulations messages to see who this mysterious guy was that she was engaged to, outside of me, when my screen updated.

I scrunched my face.

"Huh?" I reloaded the screen and searched Nicole's page, but the status had been deleted. She was now back to Single, and she posted a broken heart.

"Oh no!" I covered my mouth with my hand.

I had to find her.

Chapter 22

Zakari

Nicole went to work from eight in the morning to five in the afternoon. Her car was easy to spot, despite the massive hospital parking lot.

I watched as her beautiful curls bounced up and down while she made her way to her car. I couldn't wait to surprise her with my presence.

I couldn't do it here, though. I waited until she pulled out, then let a few other cars leave out too before making my exit.

I wasn't worried about losing her because the tracker underneath her car was working properly. It was easy to install. All I had to do was pop it in, and it was on.

I felt like I was in a detective movie as I followed her through my tracker's navigation system. She was a few streets ahead, but then she stopped moving. Probably parked somewhere. I drove past the grocery store she stopped at, then circled around to a side street to wait until she came out.

She emerged ten minutes later with a bag in her hands. I pulled around to the main street and found a space near hers in the lot, getting out of my car just as she approached hers.

"Nicole?" My eyes widened, and when she saw me, hers did, too.

"Zakari?"

I broke out in a huge smile. I couldn't help it. "Long time no see! What a surprise!"

She smiled, too. I knew she would be happy to see me. "Yes, it has been a long time."

We stood there for a few moments. "Can I get a hug?"

She blinked as if she was snapping out of a trance. This was probably a dream come true for her, too. "Sure!" She extended her arms, and I wrapped her up. She smelled good, like Chanel perfume. One of the girls I dated in college was obsessed with Chanel perfume. Lester's wife, Michelle, loved Chanel, too. What a coincidence.

"Zakari, I can't believe I'm seeing you right now," Nicole said when we pulled back from the hug.

"Me either. And you know what's crazy? I was just thinking about you yesterday. I know we lost touch, but I saw your status update to Engaged."

I tried to keep the disappointment out of my tone when I spoke, but I wasn't sure if I did a good job.

Nicole's face fell. "Yeah..."

I crossed my arms. "So, who's the lucky guy?"

She snorted. "There isn't one anymore."

My heart leapt with excitement. There was still hope. "Oh really? Why not?"

She shook her head. "Long story."

I reached out to touch her arm. "You know, Nicole, you can talk to me. We go way back."

She nodded, then was silent for a while before she spoke again. "Thank you, Zakari. I really appreciate that."

"You know what? How about we go out for coffee or something? We can catch up."

I waited with bated breath as she contemplated it.

"I guess that would be okay."

I could barely contain my excitement. "Sounds great! You have the same number, right?"

I already knew she did, since I had run a background check on her to find her new address, her job, and a few other details, but it didn't hurt to confirm.

She smiled again. "Sure do."

"Great. Well, Nicole, I won't hold you. I need to run into the store to grab some groceries."

She snapped out of her trance again. "Okay, see you later, Zakari."

"See you!" I watched as she got into her car, pulled out of her space, and drove off.

I could not wait to sweep her off her feet once again.

Chapter 23

Zakari

This Jerron character was truly a piece of work. After I got home from my meet up with Nicole, I decided to check into his background to see what I was up against.

Apparently, nothing much.

He had gone through six years of school just to get his first real job less than a week ago? No wonder Nicole called it quits. This man was a loser. Good thing they were never too serious.

I was hired at my company before I even finished my sophomore year at Wayson. Graduation and grad school were nothing more than formalities.

I was established, while this Jerron character had nothing to offer. Nicole deserved the world, and I intended to give it to her.

Not to mention that selfie he took with that woman named Shameka. I looked into her, too, and she didn't have much to offer, either. Maybe her and Jerron belonged together. They seemed like the better match.

One thing Jerron did have on me was that he was better looking. Judging from his background information, he was 6'3, while I was 6'1. He was also more muscular, judging from his pics, but I bet he wouldn't hold his own against me in a fistfight. I would fight to the finish for Nicole. He had no idea who she really was. I knew her since high school. We had longevity.

Lester called my phone, breaking me from my thoughts. "Hello?" I answered, feeling irritable. Lester always called at the wrong times.

"What's wrong with you?"

"Nothing."

He was silent for a second. "Anyway, me and Michelle wanted to know if you wanted to come over and play spades. Her girlfriend, Leslie, is supposed to come, too."

I rolled my eyes. Here Lester was again, always trying to hook me up with some woman, when I told him time and time again, I already had a woman.

He kept trying to tell me that me and Nicole weren't going to happen but look how we saw each other today. Lester never knew what he was talking about. Not back then, and certainly not now.

"Sorry, bro. I'll have to take a raincheck." I tried to let him down easily. He was, in his misguided way, trying to help, after all.

"Dang, bro. That's the third time in a row." He chuckled. "I'm starting to think it's something I said. Leslie's cute, though. You should come."

"I already have a date with Nicole." Of course, I didn't yet, but I would soon. All I had to do was call her, and it would be on. Just like high school.

"Zakari..." Lester sighed.

"What?"

"Nicole is engaged."

My eyes popped open for a second, and I was about to ask him how he knew that, then I reasoned that he must have seen her status before she changed it back.

"She's not anymore. She and I ran into each other today, and we're going to pick up where we left off."

"Zakari, that's not how it works..."

"Look, Lester, I gotta go. I have to prepare a document for my boss."

"Okay, Zakari. Talk to you later."

He hung up, sounding upset, but I didn't care. This was my life. Sooner or later, Lester would see he was wrong this whole time. Nicole and I were meant to be. It was already etched in stone.

Chapter 24

Zakari

Just to have something to show as proof to Lester, I texted Nicole.
Hey. Wyd?
Nothing much.
Wanna grab a coffee tomorrow?
There were a few minutes where she didn't answer, then she responded. *Sure.*
Are you okay?
Yes, just upset about the breakup.
I decided to call her. She needed a shoulder to cry on, just like when we were in high school, and she was crying about her parents.

"Hello?" she answered after a few rings.

"Hey. I figured you needed to talk."

She sniffled. "Zakari, I don't want to burden you."

"It's not a burden at all, Nicole. Tell me what happened."

She sighed, then fell silent. "You sure you wanna hear all this?"

"Positive."

She sniffled again, then launched into a long story of her and Jerron's relationship. I took copious notes in my pad as she spoke. Parts of her story upset me, especially the parts where she said she loved Jerron and believed he was in love with her, but I brushed it off. Clearly, he didn't love her enough if he was cheating with Shameka, and besides, the love Nicole and I shared lasted since high school. Jerron was nothing but a blip on the screen of our life together.

I waited until she was finished speaking, then offered my input. "Wow, Nicole. It sounds like Jerron put you through a lot. He had no business taking that woman's number right in front of you. Then he met up with her at a coffee shop right after he proposed? Disgusting. If you ask my opinion, you're better off without him."

She was silent for a moment. "I know, and then when I finally caught up with him, all he had were excuses."

"What kind of excuses? What explanation could he possibly have for going on a date with another woman, then turning his phone off?"

She snorted. "He claimed it wasn't a date, that they just bumped into each other. I don't believe that for one second. I don't know, Zakari. I want to believe him, but at the same time, what am I supposed to do? He deleted her number right in front of me, then ends up at a coffee shop with her the next day. Not to mention that selfie she took of them and posted on her page. I know women. She's staking her claim... Anyway, enough about me. What about you? Any women in your life?"

Only you, I wanted to say, but I knew it wasn't the time. I had to give her space to get over Jerron, then I would make my move.

"Not really," I responded. "I've been so busy with work that I haven't had time to settle down, but things are finally starting to clear up in my schedule now."

"Oh really? That's great! How is it being an engineer?"

I cleared my throat with pride, then proceeded to tell her all about my job, the salary and bonuses, benefits, and all the other perks it offered. I knew by the time I was done Nicole would see her breakup with Jerron as a blessing in disguise.

He was never the guy for her.

I was.

We talked for another hour after that, laughing and joking about old times. By the end of the conversation, Nicole was no longer crying.

Her tone was lighter, and I was thankful I was the one who put a smile on her face.

"Zakari, this was such a good conversation. We have to do this again."

"Indeed, we do," I said, already contemplating our first official date as a renewed couple.

Chapter 25

Zakari

The next day, I went to work and breezed through my shift. I could not wait to get off so I could call Nicole. I planned to take her out this weekend and remind her of what she was missing.

I hummed my favorite gospel song by Fred Hammond as I gave the voice command to my Bluetooth. She answered on the third ring in an even more upbeat tone than the one I had.

"Hey, Zakari!"

I loved the sound of my name coming from her lips. I could not wait to make her my wife.

"Hey, sweet thang."

Silence for a moment, then she replied. "What's up with you?"

"Nothing much. Just got off work. What are you up to?"

She giggled, and my heart fluttered. "I just got off work myself, but guess what?"

"What?" I asked, giggling too.

"I am such an idiot."

"An idiot how?" *For not remembering the love of your life has been waiting on you for seven years? I forgive you, baby.*

"Jerron and I had a long talk after I got off the phone with you last night."

My smile erased immediately, and I had to slam on my brakes to avoid crashing into the car in front of me.

"About what?" I tried to take the accusation out of my tone, but I couldn't help it.

"Everything was a big misunderstanding. He wasn't cheating with Shameka."

The walls were closing in on me. It was getting way too hot in my car. I twisted the knob to turn on the air conditioner. "What makes you believe he wasn't cheating?"

She sighed a happy sigh, and that was when I knew I underestimated Jerron. He apparently had a deeper hold on her than I thought. Two could play that game.

"He explained everything, and it made sense. I overreacted."

"Nicole, are you sure? What was his explanation for his phone being turned off?"

"He had to go into his new job to fill out paperwork. He mentioned it to me, but in all my anger over seeing the picture of them together, I forgot about that. I feel like such an idiot. That's what I get for overreacting."

"Nicole..." I didn't know what to say. This whole thing came out of left field. One minute, me and Nicole were back on track, but the next, Jerron reared his ugly head and snatched her away from me. This meant war.

"Yes?" she said in that loving, sweet voice I had grown to love.

"Nothing. Congratulations on your engagement."

"Thank you!" she gushed. "You're definitely invited to the wedding, too. It's going to be on June first."

"Yup, I'll be there."

We hung up, and I had to think quickly. The problem was, the more I wracked my brains, the more I couldn't think straight. I could not let Nicole marry that man. Not when we were so close. Not after I had done all the work.

This had to be a test or a trial. Maybe both.

I pulled up to our house and sat in the driveway. Something had to give.

My phone buzzed with a notification. I swiped the screen to check it, and Nicole had updated her status again.

This wasn't fair.

I stared at the background picture on my phone. I updated it after me and Nicole's first phone conversation to a selfie we took together back in high school.

Something clicked in my mind, and I felt a sense of calm. Jerron had to be taken down, and I now knew just how to do it. He could not have my woman.

I had to save her from him.

Chapter 26

Nicole

I was an idiot. I felt so stupid blowing things out of proportion and changing my status, getting everybody all confused, just to change it right back two days later. Maybe I should get off social media for a while. I laughed it off in my re-engagement post, saying the broken engagement was a false alarm, and people laughed with me, but I knew in the back of their minds they thought I was crazy.

Heck, I didn't blame them.

I guess with all the stress associated with Jerron taking so long to set a date for our wedding, to seeing how he acted around Shameka, to finally getting a wedding date, to seeing that picture Shareese sent me of them together, not to mention Shameka taking a picture herself and uploading it on her page... I felt so dumb.

Never again. I usually wasn't this impulsive.

Was I being desperate because I wanted so badly for me and Jerron's relationship to work? Maybe I was. The one good thing that came out of this whole situation was that me and Zakari reconnected. We had lost touch a couple of years ago, but he had always been a good friend to me.

He saw me one time after me and Jerron broke up and was ready to be a shoulder to cry on. Words could not express my appreciation for him for doing that. He didn't have to sit there for hours with me, encouraging me about my relationship with Jerron. I had to get

Zakari a card or something. Maybe a nice gift to show my thankfulness.

Anywho, I had a wedding to plan - again.

I needed to call Shareese to update her. I was sure her head was spinning like mine was with the twisted turn of events.

"Hello?" she answered. "Nicole, I just saw your status. What's up with you?"

I opened my mouth to answer her, but I didn't like the tone she used in her question. What did she mean, what was up with me? Why'd she say it like that?

Now that I thought of it, Shareese wasn't one of the people who laughed with me on my false alarm post. She also only *liked* my original engagement update, while other people *hearted* it. What was up with that?

Calm down, Nicole. No more jumping to conclusions, my mind told me.

"Girl, I am such a fool." I sighed.

"What happened?"

"First and foremost, I'm sorry for the way I talked to you the other day when you sent that picture. I hung up in your face, and that was wrong."

"Girl, I'm not upset about that. I understood you were caught off guard."

"Thank you. Secondly, Jerron and I are back together. He wasn't cheating with Shameka after all."

"What?" Shareese's tone was incredulous. Why did she sound so shocked? Not to mention disappointed. It was no secret that Shareese never liked Jerron, and the feelings were mutual on his end. I had no idea what that was about, but since they tolerated each other for my sake, I left it alone.

"Nope, he wasn't cheating. I overreacted." I explained to her what happened.

"And you believed him, huh?" she said after I finished.

"Yes, why?"

Shareese sighed. "Nicole, listen. I'm not trying to tell you how to live your life, but you need to use better discernment."

My ears grew hot. "Better discernment?"

"Yes. He goes on a date with a woman the day after you got engaged, after you told him you weren't comfortable with their friendship, then he allows her to take a selfie of them? Don't be stupid, Nicole."

"I'm not stupid, Shareese." I held a warning in my tone. She needed to back off before I spilled her tea like she thought she was spilling mine.

"I'm not calling you stupid. I'm looking out for you as a friend. It's one thing to have a simple misunderstanding and another to let a man take you for a fool."

"And you would know the difference, huh?" I couldn't help but to retort. I had hit below the belt, I knew it, but I wasn't about to sit there and let her talk to me like that. Especially when she just got back with Vance, her on again, off again boyfriend of four years.

"What's that supposed to mean?"

"You and Vance."

"Nicole, me and Vance are not the same as you and Jerron. We have a child together."

"Despite your child, he cheated on you for real."

It was true. Shareese caught Vance coming out of one of his women's houses the first time they broke up.

"Listen, I gotta go. I'll talk to you later." Shareese hung up before I had a chance to say anything else. I wasn't upset about it, though. She wanted to get on me so bad, calling me desperate over Jerron, who wasn't even cheating, when she had a whole baby daddy who admitted to cheating three times.

Later that night, conviction started eating at me. I shouldn't have brought up Shareese and Vance's relationship. It was uncalled for, and she was only trying to help. There I went again. It seemed like I couldn't win for losing these days.

Why was I flying off the handle lately?

Was me and Jerron's relationship causing me to become a bad person?

I didn't want to hurt Shareese. She was my day one. I had to make this right.

Hey, girl, I texted. *I am so sorry for everything I said earlier. There is no excuse, and it won't happen again.*

She responded a few minutes later. *You're fine. I probably am stupid for taking Vance back again, but I love him, Nicole.*

I felt her pain through her text. I called her immediately.

"Hello?" she answered in tears.

"Hey, girl. Listen, do you want me to come over?"

She sniffled. "No, you're good. I'm just emotional because... I'm pregnant again."

My jaw dropped. "Again? Is that why you took him back this time?"

"Yes." Her voice wavered as she spoke. "He told me he was changing. He promised."

Vance promised the last three times, but I wasn't about to bring that up.

"You know I'm here for you, girl, no matter how it turns out."

"Same here. I wish you and Jerron the best."

My heart softened when she said that because Shareese did not like Jerron.

"Thank you. You're gonna be my maid of honor, right?"

"Of course, girl! You're gonna be mine if me and Vance get that far?"

"You don't even have to ask."

We shared a laugh, then chatted for a few more moments before calling it a night.

Chapter 27

Nicole

I was floating on cloud nine over the course of the next week. Jerron and I were back on track, Shareese was helping me with the wedding planning, and Mike and Tina's wedding was coming up in a few short weeks.

Life was going to be a blur for the next couple of months, but I was here for it.

Less than ninety days before I became Mrs. Davis.

I submitted my paperwork for time off for two weeks after me and Jerron's wedding. We hadn't settled on a honeymoon location yet, but I wanted us to have ample time to get to know each other as husband and wife.

Matter of fact, we needed to choose a location tonight. I wanted to ensure we booked our flight and hotel well ahead of time to get the best deals. I was just about to hit the button to call Jerron on my dashboard when a call came in from Zakari.

"Hey!" I answered, happy to hear from him. I still had to get him a card for his nice gesture.

"Hey, Nicole. How are things?"

"They're good. Just getting everything ready for this wedding. How are you?"

He coughed. "I'm good. Just working. Maintaining."

"Yeah?" I turned down a side street. "Work must be busy for you, huh?" I remembered him telling me how the company he worked for was expanding.

"Actually, I..."

A call beeped in from Jerron, and my heart skipped a beat. "Zakari, let me call you back later. Jerron is beeping in."

"Okay," he said, and we hung up.

"Hello?" I answered Jerron's call.

"Hey, lady," his smooth voice filled my vehicle. A passion ignited within me just by hearing him talk. I couldn't wait until we could fully let loose in our feelings for one another.

"How are you today?" I asked.

"I'm good. I wanted to stop by tonight so we could talk about a location for our honeymoon."

A smile grew across my face. "I was literally about to call you and say the same thing, but I got distracted."

"Distracted, huh? By what?"

"My high school sweetheart," I teased.

"Oh boy, here we go." He chuckled. "You leaving me for him?"

"Only if you don't act right," I flirted.

"I guess I better be on the straight and narrow then."

"You better. You still got a lot of making up to do for your prior infractions."

"I'll make it up over these next few months and do overtime once we get married."

He switched to a lower tone when he said that last part.

"Overtime, huh?" My face flushed as I envisioned exactly what he meant by that statement.

"Yes, we might need at least a month to ourselves."

Jerron's seductiveness was almost too much for me. I was ready to move the wedding date up and elope over the weekend or something.

"Watch yourself, now!" I joked.

"I prefer watching you."

I giggled, then he switched back to his regular tone. "Anyway, I'm on my way, woman. You want me to bring you anything?"

"Hm, maybe some KFC." I loved their chicken and hadn't had any in a while.

"Your wish is my command. I'm about to pull into the drive thru."

I thought he was joking until I heard the lady's voice come through the intercom asking what he wanted to order. I told her my order, and Jerron told her his, then he was at my apartment five minutes after I arrived.

I greeted him with a kiss at the door, though our flirt session from earlier had me wanting to do much more.

Only ninety more days, I reminded myself.

Chapter 28

Nicole

I should have known my happiness wasn't going to last long.

Shareese called me from the hospital, crying in pain because she lost her and Vance's new baby. I immediately rushed there and sat with her for hours until he could get there. He came in all sweaty, saying he came straight there from making an out-of-town delivery for his job. I wasn't sure that was believable, even though he was wearing his uniform, but I didn't say anything. He did race to her side, though, taking over in comforting her. Vance seemed genuinely sad they lost the baby.

I hoped that meant he was serious about changing for the better this time.

Unfortunately, my bad day only got worse from there.

On my way home, I got a call from a random number.

I answered, thinking nothing of it because I submitted my phone number to multiple places looking for quotes on venues and such.

"Hello?" I answered in my professional voice. "This is Nicole speaking. May I ask who's calling?"

I pulled over and got ready to take notes on whatever the company was about to tell me.

A female voice sounded through my speakers.

It wasn't a company.

"Hi, Nicole. This is Shameka."

I sat there, unsure of how to continue the conversation. "Okay... How did you get my number? And why are you calling?"

"I couldn't help but see that you updated your status the other day."

I felt my ears growing hot, and dread filled my stomach. "Yes, I did. And?"

There was a brief pause before she continued. "Listen, Nicole, there isn't an easy way to say this, especially since we don't know each other, but I thought you should know what type of guy Jerron is before you marry him."

My ears pricked up. What was she talking about? "I think I know what type of man Jerron is, honey. We've been together for seven years."

"Off and on, I know. You dated in college but didn't get serious until grad school."

That threw me for a loop, especially with how her tone changed during that last part, like she was being sarcastic. How did she know anything about me and Jerron's relationship?

"Shameka, please stop playing on my phone."

"I'm not playing. I called to tell you that not only did me and Jerron date all through your college years during your off times, but we also never stopped seeing each other."

"That's impossible!" I spat before I could stop myself. I couldn't let her know she was getting under my skin.

Too late.

"It's actually quite possible, honey. He probably didn't mention this to you, but we have a child together."

My jaw dropped. She was lying. This was not true.

"I don't believe you."

"Okay. See for yourself."

A few seconds later, my phone buzzed three times. I didn't want to check the notification, but I had to.

When I did, my heart sank. There it was, Shameka holding a baby. The baby was the spitting image of Jerron. The other two pictures were of the child as a toddler, then what I assumed to be a recent photo. In each picture, it was undeniable. It was Jerron's child.

"His name is Mario," Shameka's voice cut in again. "Jerron hasn't been an active force in his life because he was too busy playing around with you, but I'm not doing that anymore. I'm going to put him on child support. Also, I don't plan to stop seeing him, so you can either get out of my way or plan to have me as a sister-wife for the rest of your life."

I hung up the phone.

It was too much for me.

This was the final straw.

I shook uncontrollably, overcome with emotion as a flood of tears overtook me. I cried so hard I had to open my car door and throw up on the street.

A dagger to my heart.

This whole time I thought me and Jerron would be together forever.

And he had a whole child. A whole life with another woman.

In my heart of hearts, I didn't want to believe it, but I couldn't deny the proof. I stared at those photos until my screen went black.

I didn't know what to do.

Chapter 29

Nicole

I decided to spare myself the anguish and make me and Jerron's breakup as smooth as possible. *I never want to see or hear from you again,* I texted. *Tell Shameka she can have you. I'm done.* Then I blocked him and Shameka in case she tried to call again to rub it in my face.

I deactivated my social media accounts.

Numb. That was how I felt. Numb and dumb, dumb and numb. Thoughts swirled in my mind, dancing in a tango of emotion.

I wanted to kill him.

All that time, all those signs, and I stuck by him. I should have known he was a liar. Now that I thought of it, I was the biggest fool on the planet. He prolonged our wedding for a year because he didn't have a job? BS. That didn't stop him from proposing. Then he sat there and exchanged numbers with Shameka right in front of me, then tried to play stupid like he didn't see how that was disrespectful. And I believed him. I gave him the benefit of doubt and look where I was.

I hated Shameka, too, for sucking the joy out of me, but at the same time, I knew she had done me a favor. I would have stayed with my head in the clouds until after me and Jerron got married. What would I have done if I found out about the child after we tied the knot? That would have certainly been more devastating.

A call came in from Shareese. "Hello?"

"Hey, girl!" she said in a chipper tone. "Guess what?"

"What?" I didn't try to hide the depression in my voice.

"What's wrong?"

"Nothing," I said, then burst into a fresh round of tears.

"Oh no, Nicole, what happened?" Shareese sounded like she was tearing up, too.

"Jerron cheated!" I wailed, then I forwarded the pictures to her phone.

There was a moment of silence as she viewed them, then she said, "I'm coming over."

When she got to my apartment, she immediately swept me up in a hug. "Nicole, I'm so sorry." When we pulled back, she was wiping tears from her own face just like I was.

"I should have believed you when you told me he was no good," I mumbled, but a knock on my front door interrupted us.

"Who is it?" I yelled, immediately filled with anger. I yanked open the door, and Jerron was standing there having the nerve to look confused.

"Go away!" I shouted.

"Nicole? Baby, what's going on?" He tried to enter my apartment, but I roughly pushed him backward, Shareese at my side with a steely gaze of her own.

Jerron stared at us like he was shocked. "What is this? What happened? I get this random text from you, then you blocked me..."

"Cut the charade, Jerron! I'm not your fool anymore!" I boomed loud enough for the whole neighborhood to hear.

"Nicole, I don't know what you're talking about."

Shareese sucked her teeth. "Come on, Jerron. She knows about Shameka and the baby."

"Baby?" Jerron blinked. "What the hell are you..."

"Don't try to deny it! I saw the pictures, you liar! You have a four-year-old son. Don't you dare try to stand there and tell me you don't know what I'm talking about."

I swore, if he lied to me again, it was on. I was going to swing on him.

"Nicole, I swear I don't..."

He didn't get a chance to finish because I was on him like white on rice. He tried to block me as I rained blows all over his face, head, and shoulders.

"Nicole!" Shareese said, trying to break us up, but I was too wild to be stopped.

I felt a crunch underneath my feet as I continued to hit him everywhere my fists could land. That must have been his glasses. Oops.

I heard sirens approaching, but I didn't care.

Finally, Jerron was able to grab my wrists as the police were turning the corner to my street.

"Nicole..." he panted, trying to catch his breath. There was blood coming down from his left eye and his bottom lip, but I didn't care.

"I gave you seven years!" I hissed. "Seven years!"

I wrenched my arms away from him as the police car pulled up in front of my house.

"Sir? Ma'am? What's going on?" the officer said as he approached.

It was at that moment I realized I was about to go to jail. I looked at Shareese, ready to tell her to call my mother to bail me out.

"Nothing, officer," Jerron cut in.

The officer peered at his bloody face. "Sir, are you hurt?"

"No, I'm fine. It's just a misunderstanding."

The officer looked at me. "Did you hit him?"

I opened my mouth to answer, but Jerron cut him off.

"No, she didn't do anything. I fell."

The officer's brows furrowed. "You fell, huh?"

"Yes, nothing happened, and I'm not pressing charges. I'm leaving now. This situation is over."

We all watched as Jerron walked to his car as if he was in a daze, started it up, and drove off.

The officer stared at Jerron's departing vehicle, then back at me. "Ma'am, it's clear to me that he didn't fall and cause those injuries to himself."

I swallowed.

"But since he's not pressing charges, I'm not going to waste my time," he continued. "If I'm called here again, though, I'm arresting you both."

I nodded to say I understood, then he looked at Shareese.

"Thank you, Officer," she said. "We're going inside now." She gently grabbed my arm.

The officer nodded and walked back to his vehicle as me and Shareese headed back inside my apartment. I knew I was going to hear from my landlord about this because my neighbors were the nosey type. Part of me didn't care.

My mind hadn't fully caught up to what happened yet.

All I knew was my heart was shattered, and this was only the beginning of my pain.

Chapter 30

Nicole

I didn't leave my house for three days after what happened. I went through multiple boxes of Kleenex, but crying did nothing to soothe me. Jerron had broken me.

He came knocking at the door again the next day, but I didn't answer.

Then he called me from Mike's phone, and I blocked Mike, too.

Tina tried to reach out, and I held a polite conversation with her, but by the end, I made sure she understood I wanted no parts of Jerron.

I mailed the ring back to him on day four.

That was the first thing I did when I exited my apartment for the first time.

Part of me wanted to pawn it for my troubles, but the other part wanted this situation over with. Good riddance. Seven years down the drain, but at least I didn't have to deal with a lifetime of baby momma drama.

I went to work with my head held high, keeping up with the lie I told my boss about missing a few days due to food poisoning.

They handed me a Get-Well card signed by all the staff, and I almost burst into tears right then. I was not okay.

I would be, though… as soon as I got over Jerron.

I pushed him to the back of my mind and powered through my shift. I even held a smile on my face, to the point where I almost convinced myself that everything was fine.

When I got back to my car and saw Jerron standing beside it, however, I realized how dangerously close I was to losing my mind.

"What are you doing here?" I gritted through my teeth.

"Nicole, we need to talk." The swelling in Jerron's lip had gone down, his eye was healing, and he had gotten new glasses, but none of that mattered to me. I meant what I said when I said we were through. Still, I decided to entertain this last conversation with him as a formality. I had a feeling he would never go away if I didn't.

"What do you want, Jerron?"

He studied me. "Can we go sit somewhere?"

"No, I'm fine standing right here. Hurry up with your speech, though, because I need to get home."

He took a step back like I wounded him, but I didn't care. He wounded me way worse because I didn't see this coming.

I never knew our relationship would end like this.

I always pegged Jerron for a standup guy.

"Why propose to me when you had a whole baby mother?" I demanded before I could realize I was speaking.

Jerron sighed. "Nicole, I have no idea what Shameka told you, but I don't have any child with her. I have no children."

"That's funny, because the three photos of a child who could be your twin were sent to my phone. Any other lies you want to rack up?"

He gave me a perplexed look. "What photos?"

I rolled my eyes. "The photos of your son, Mario, Jerron. Let's not play this game."

"Nicole, I'm not playing any games, I swear. I have no idea why Shameka is lying like this suddenly. I haven't seen her for almost ten years, so how do I have a four-year-old child with her?"

"Ding ding, another lie! She told me about how you guys saw each other while we were in college."

"That's not true!" he sputtered. "Nicole, you really believe this?"

"What do you think, Jerron? I'm going to stand here and believe your lies again and take you back again, just for you to take me for a fool... again? Why don't you go be with your baby momma?"

"I don't have a baby mother!" he thundered.

I blinked. That was it for me. I clicked my fob to get into my car.

"Nicole, wait. I'll get a DNA test to prove it."

"No need. I should have taken the first sign as confirmation and ran. You strung me along for a whole year after you proposed, and now I know why."

"I told you why!" He grabbed my arm as I opened my driver's side door.

I wrenched away. "I suggest you refrain from ever touching me again. If you show up to my job again, I'm filing for a restraining order."

He stood there and watched at my door as I slammed it, then clicked my seatbelt.

"Nicole!" he rapped on my window as I turned the key in the ignition.

I slid the window down, ready to be done with this conversation.

Tears filled his eyes, and I had to look away to not get caught up in his trance. "You're really not going to give me a chance to prove myself to you?"

"Nope."

"Nicole..."

"Yes, Jerron?" I mustered up a sarcastic tone and expression to get him away from me.

His Adam's apple bobbed up and down as he swallowed. "This is really it between us?"

"Yup, it's really it." He was annoying me now, putting on this act like he was so sad, when the whole time he was playing me behind my back with Shameka.

The Lord must have orchestrated us running into her at the mall that day. I would have to find a way to thank Him later. It hurt, but I knew it was for my good.

"Okay," he finally said, his voice hoarse like he was a broken man.

I sucked my teeth and pressed the gas pedal to back the hell away from him. I was done with Jerron's lies and manipulation. Shameka could live her life as a sister-wife, but I sure wasn't. If Jerron couldn't be satisfied with one woman, he wasn't the man for me, simple as that.

Chapter 31

Nicole

Thirty excruciating days went by, and Jerron honored my wishes. He left me alone. I should have felt happy, relieved that he was letting me move on with my life, but instead, I felt a range of emotions, none of them good.

I barely ate or slept. I snapped at people. I ignored phone calls and text messages and kept conversations short when I did respond.

Every day, I told myself I was over Jerron, but every night, I wondered if he moved on with Shameka.

All my thoughts of him must have summoned the devil because I saw Mike and Tina walking hand in hand when I went to the grocery store one day.

"Nicole!" Tina said when she saw me.

I wanted to dodge the conversation, especially since I blocked Mike and never showed up to their wedding, but I knew I couldn't.

"Hey." I wracked my brains for an excuse to bolt to my car.

Mike had a serious expression on his face. He wasted no time getting to his point. "Jerron's distraught over you guys' breakup."

I didn't have time for this, to stand here and listen to him back up a liar and a cheater. "Oh yeah? Tell him to have Shameka console him. Maybe spend a little time with his son. That should ease his broken heart."

I didn't bother to hide my sarcasm or bitterness.

Tina cut in. "Nicole, Jerron doesn't have a son."

I rolled my eyes. She was drinking the Kool-Aid, too?

"Tina, come on now. I saw the pictures. Let's not do this."

"What pictures?" they said in unison, as if this were the first time they heard of such a thing. That was when I realized Jerron had them fooled, too. They weren't taking up for him. He lied to them just like he lied to me!

Wow, Jerron was a piece of work. I had been so depressed about our relationship ending, but now I realized he didn't deserve my emotions.

If he could sit there and lie to his best friends about a child he refused to claim, why would I ever think he would give me an ounce of decency?

"I wish I could show you, but I deleted the pictures from my phone. He's definitely Jerron's, though. He looked exactly like him."

Mike appeared to be taken aback. "I'm sure this is just a misunderstanding, Nicole. If you would just give him a chance to explain…"

"You can't explain a child away, Mike. You know that."

My eyes shot to Tina, who was now silent. She nodded as if she agreed with me. "Mike, let her go." She turned back to me. "Nicole, I understand where you're coming from. If you ever need to talk, I still want to be your friend. Feel free to reach out."

"I sure will," I lied. There was no way I was reaching out to her, at least not for a while. Tina was cool, but I only knew her through my connection to Jerron. I wanted no parts of anyone or anything associated with him at the moment.

Maybe once my feelings died down.

I said my final goodbye to my former friends, went through the checkout, then headed home. When I got there, I called Shareese to tell her what happened.

"Girl, can you believe he lied to them, too?"

Shareese was silent.

"Shareese?" I pulled the phone away from my ear to make sure the call hadn't disconnected. It hadn't.

"Nicole..." her voice trailed off.

Something was wrong.

My heart sank. I could not deal with any more bad news, yet I braced myself for the worst. "What is it?"

"I have something to tell you."

I sighed. Might as well hear it now, whatever it was. "Go ahead."

"It's about Jerron... and me. About why we never got along."

Oh, God... Shareese was about to tell me she slept with Jerron, too. If she did, I was going to his house tonight to finish that beatdown.

"What is it, Shareese?" I stood and began to pace the floor, my mind swimming with possibilities.

"I wanted to tell you this before, but it never seemed like the right time."

"You slept together?" I blurted before she could continue.

"What? No!" she said as if she was disgusted, and I calmed. *Thank God.*

"Okay... what happened, then?"

"Listen..." She sighed. "Before you and Jerron met in freshman year, we dated, briefly."

My jaw dropped. "You dated? You and Jerron?"

"Yes. We went out together, and I thought we were going somewhere, then he ghosted me."

"He ghosted you?" My mind was reeling as I tried to wrap my mind around what Shareese was telling me.

"It shouldn't have meant anything, but when I found out you were dating him a month later, I was pissed. I confronted him, and we got into a huge argument. I planned to tell you about what happened, but you seemed so happy with him, I decided against it."

"So, you and Jerron dated before me and him got together, and neither of you told me about it."

"It's not like we slept together, but yes. I'm sorry, Nicole."

I didn't know what to think of that. Mystery solved, I guessed. They hadn't slept together, or at least Shareese said they didn't, but still...

"You know what?" I blurted. "I'm not going to even bother myself about that revelation."

"You sure? I know I should have told you."

"Yup, I'm sure. I accept your apology. Me and Jerron are through, anyway, and I don't have the mental bandwidth to keep up with any more of his lies."

"I'm sorry, Nicole. Seriously."

"You're good, Shareese." She wasn't, but I would get over it eventually.

Life was chock-full of surprises lately.

The next day, I decided to join a gym. I needed a place to let out all my angst and put my best foot forward to get over Jerron.

He hadn't tried to reach back out to me, so he was probably happily back with Shameka. It was for the best, anyway, seeing that Mario needed his father.

I took a spinning class and although it was for beginners, my body was drenched with sweat when I finished, not to mention releasing tons of endorphins.

That was just what I needed.

I found myself humming as I took a quick shower to get the stink off me, then headed out the door with lifted spirits.

On my way across the parking lot, I ran into Zakari.

"Wow! Second time I've seen you in a matter of months!" I said as we shared a hug.

"Hey, Nicole! You got your workout on?" He smiled that goofy smile I remembered from years ago.

"Yup!" I beamed, proud of myself that I wasn't letting heartache hold me back.

"You look great," he said.

"Thank you. That's an extra special compliment, seeing that I just joined."

Zakari nodded like he was surprised. "Wow, you just joined and you're already glowing? Keep it up, woman!"

We shared a lighthearted laugh. "Listen, Zakari," I said, touching his elbow as I spoke. "It was good seeing you, but my legs are killing me. I'm about to head home and crash for the night."

Zakari chuckled. "You have a good night then."

I turned back toward my car, but Zakari called out for me again. "Nicole?"

I faced him.

"You mind if I call you later tonight?" He stopped himself. "If that's okay with Jerron, of course."

My face fell, and once again, my emotions were all over the place. I forced another smile to my face as I looked back up at him. "It's fine. You can call."

He didn't seem to notice the change in my demeanor. "Cool!" He headed toward the gym, and I entered my vehicle, then headed home.

Chapter 32

Zakari

I watched from the doors of the gym as Nicole pulled out of the parking lot, then when she was a safe distance away, I headed back to my car.

It was a good sign that she acquired a membership. It meant she was getting over Jerron.

I smiled and hummed an old school gospel tune as I turned the key in my ignition. *"Jesus getting us ready for that great day..."* I double-clapped my hands along with the imaginary beat in my head and broke out in full song mode. *"Jesus getting us ready for that great day... Jesus getting us ready for that great day! Who shall be able to stand?"*

I knew my great day with Nicole was soon to come.

I would call her tomorrow instead of tonight, just so I wouldn't seem desperate, and we would have our first official date this weekend.

It was time.

No more waiting.

No more lamenting over Jerron.

He was never the man for her, anyway, she would see.

Later that night, I prepared myself a meal of tiny red potatoes, baked chicken, and asparagus. I spent the past month learning to cook as I awaited the time to reconnect with Nicole. Now that it was here, I could see my hard work finally starting to pay off.

I wondered if this was how Jacob felt when he finally got Rachel.

First, he got tricked into messing with that ugly duckling, Leah, but finally, the Lord smiled upon his situation.

I had my own ugly ducklings as I awaited Nicole, my swan, and she had her ugly duckling in Jerron.

Now it was time for us to embark on our journey toward forever.

I was lost in thought for a moment before being rudely interrupted by a phone call from Lester. He always picked the wrong times.

"Hello?"

"Hey, man, why do you always answer with an attitude?"

"Nothing. What do you want?"

He paused. "Dang, is this a bad time?"

"I'm in the middle of dinner."

"Okay... I'll call back later, then."

"Cool."

He didn't hang up. "You sure you good, man?"

I changed my tone. "Yeah, man. Just hungry. Went to the gym earlier."

"Oh, I didn't know you had a membership! Which gym?"

"Heights of Fitness."

"That new one up on Chelsea Street? I heard it was nice."

"It is."

"Wow, I might get a membership myself. Michelle complained about me putting on a few pounds." He chuckled.

I laughed politely with him, but on the inside, I couldn't wait until he shut up so I could hang up and focus my thoughts back on Nicole.

"Alright, Zakari. I'll let you get back to your dinner. Hit me tomorrow, okay?"

"Okay."

I hung up with Lester, then finished my meal.

I could not wait for tomorrow morning to come, so I could call Nicole.

Chapter 33

Nicole

It seemed like I was seeing Zakari more and more lately. It was crazy how just when my relationship with Jerron was on its last leg, my friendship with Zakari ramped back up.

Maybe that was a sign.

Zakari had always been cool. I just wasn't ready for a serious relationship when we were in high school. Funny how the tables turned when it came to Jerron.

A thought came to me... Did I have to go through what I went through with Jerron because of what I did to Zakari? I hadn't meant to string him along, but some would probably argue that I did.

Jerron had done the same to me. I was reaping what I had sown.

As that thought passed through my mind, Zakari called.

"Hello?" I answered.

"Hey, Nicole! How are things?"

"I'm good." I readjusted myself in my seat. "How are you?"

"Good... listen, I've been thinking, we never got to grab that cup of coffee a while back. Are you still up for it? My fault about the delay, work's been crazy."

My heart jumped. "Uh yeah, sure! Coffee would be great!"

"Glad to hear it. I'm about to head in for my shift now, but I'll see you Saturday?"

"Saturday it is." I beamed.

"Cool, can't wait."

When we hung up, I got to thinking again... Maybe God wasn't punishing me by having me go through heartache with Jerron. Maybe He was setting me up to be with Zakari! It made perfect sense. When we were younger, we were cool, and Zakari was always my shoulder to cry on when I was going through hard times. I had been that person for him too, we just weren't ready for anything deeper. Now we were grown and more established. Maybe God meant for us to find each other again in adulthood.

I needed to call Shareese to run this idea by her. She was neutral toward Zakari, unlike her relationship with Jerron. Yet another sign.

I was getting excited, then I stopped myself.

I was jumping the gun again.

Maybe I was desperate. That was probably what the Lord was trying to show me above all. Why did I have such a need to be married? Was it because Mike and Tina tied the knot? Or the fact that I'd seen so many relationships that didn't work that I wanted to prove that one could? My mom and dad had gotten divorced. Shareese's parents did, too. I was surrounded by broken relationships. Maybe I was harping on marriage because I wanted to make a difference.

I decided to give myself more time to heal from my relationship with Jerron and build a friendship with Zakari in the meantime.

I would let the Lord show me where He wanted us to go.

Chapter 34

Nicole

The next day, I woke up feeling uneasy about going for coffee with Zakari. I didn't know why, but I did. Was it because I still felt loyalty toward Jerron?

I shouldn't, especially since he wasn't loyal to me.

My gut told me that wasn't it, it was something else, but another side of me felt like I was jumping to conclusions. Zakari was my friend.

We knew each other for half our lives. Why not go for a coffee with him?

What harm could it be?

I stopped by my mom's house after leaving work to visit with her and mention my upcoming date with Zakari. She was there when me and Zakari were together during high school. Maybe she would have insight about what I should do.

"Hey, Mom!" I greeted her as I walked in and kicked off my shoes, then placed them on the shoe rack that sat near the front door.

My mom was a stickler for being neat and tidy. I ran my apartment the same way she did our house while I was growing up. I couldn't leave dishes in the sink or the floor un-swept or the bathroom uncleaned. My mom drilled cleanliness into me.

Guess it paid off.

"Hi, Nicole. What brings you here?" We shared a hug, then I followed her to the kitchen where she was making steak and mashed potatoes. My mouth was watering from the delicious aromas.

"I sensed you were cooking steak," I joked. "No, I wanted to ask you something."

I watched as my mom finished cooking, then fixed our plates.

We sat down and said Grace, then she let out a comfortable breath. "What did you want to talk to me about?"

I took another bite, then sat back in my seat. "Zakari."

She wrinkled her nose. "Zakari? Your friend from high school? What about him?"

My ears grew hot. "We ran into each other a few times recently."

My mother studied me. "Seen each other in what context?"

"Just randomly, but I'm thinking it might mean something."

She rested her chin in her palm. "What do you think it means?"

I blushed. "Maybe I was supposed to be with him instead of Jerron."

There. I said it. Now that it was out, Mom could tell me what to do.

She sighed. "Nicole, I don't think you're ready for another relationship, especially not with Zakari. He was a little overwhelming when you were with him before, wasn't he?"

My eyes widened. "How did you know that?" I had never told my mother about my issues with Zakari.

"I heard you on the phone with Shareese a few times. Plus, I made my own observations. You didn't have to tell me."

I fell silent. She was right, but... That was back then. I was just a kid. I was a grown woman now, and Zakari was a grown man.

As if she was reading my mind, Mom said, "You can handle it however you wish, but I think you should wait. Give yourself time to heal. If you ask me, the jury's still out for Jerron."

My jaw dropped. "Jerron?"

My mother nodded. "Yes, Jerron. It was clear to me you were in love with him. I never saw you feel that way about Zakari."

"Mom, Jerron cheated on me."

"Says his random ex."

"I saw the pictures..."

She held her hand up. "When a woman wants something, she knows how to get it, Nicole. Trust me, I know."

What was that supposed to mean? I wanted to ask her, but then I didn't. I came here for advice, but I felt like my mom wasn't giving Zakari a fair chance. Yes, I made complaints in high school, but things were different now.

"Okay, Mom," I said, resuming my meal. "Thank you."

Chapter 35

Nicole

Mom was wrong. Zakari and I went out for coffee that Saturday, and we had been joined at the hip ever since. It had only been two weeks, but still.

It was as if me and Zakari had a deeper connection than ever before. He anticipated my every desire. When I entered the coffee shop, he surprised me with a cup of coffee exactly the way I took it. How could he have known? That was sexy, something that Jerron had never done.

He pulled out my seat for me before I sat down, then pushed it to the table. It was weird at first, then I felt like a lady. Zakari was pulling out all the stops to make sure I felt special. There was no question about his intentions to make me his woman, and if he was giving me this type of energy for the first two weeks of us getting reacquainted with one another, who knew what was coming?

Of course, I knew people tended to put their best foot forward in the beginning, so I wasn't going into this thing blindly, but I was definitely taking notes. Zakari was checking all the right boxes.

After my fifth date with Zakari, I was floating on cloud nine. He called into a radio show and won us concert tickets to see my favorite gospel artist, Jonathan McReynolds. We had a great time. Zakari and I sang along with all the songs and even got to take a picture with Jonathan after it was over.

I had never experienced anything like that before.

"Hope you had a good time," Zakari said with fire and desire in his eyes.

Butterflies filled my stomach. "I sure did!"

He leaned over to kiss me, but a horn honked behind us, interrupting the moment. We were at a drive thru picking up a quick meal and had gotten caught up in the nostalgia.

Zakari chuckled, and I giggled as we moved forward. We ordered our food, then he brought me home, and we chatted late into the evening in the parking lot in front of my apartment. When it was time to go, I didn't want the night to end.

I yawned. "Zakari, it is almost two o'clock in the morning. I gotta get to bed if I plan on working tomorrow... or today, rather."

His lids were low as well. "Same here. See you again soon." He leaned over and kissed my cheek, then I got out to go inside.

I couldn't wait to see him again.

The next day, I went to work bright and early as usual. Surprisingly, I wasn't as tired as I thought I would be, despite spending half the night outside with Zakari.

Who would have thought one day we would pick back up where we left off like this?

I went through my shift with ease, but when I got to my car in the parking lot, things took a downward turn.

Jerron was leaning against his vehicle, which was parked next to mine.

He straightened up as I approached him. "Hey." He gave me an uneasy stare, like he was afraid to engage with me.

I sighed, and an indiscernible feeling arose within me. I knew I would see him again sooner or later, but now wasn't the right moment. I was almost over him, I swore to myself, but my emotions were beginning to betray me. Everything I locked behind the doors in my mind was threatening to resurface. Why did life have to be so hard?

"Hey." I answered in a short tone and crossed my arms in hopes that this conversation would end quickly. My heart rate increased, but I refused to be happy to see him. Or to notice that he seemed to have built a few more muscles since we last saw each other. Or to zero in on the perfect wave pattern in his hair I had grown to love over the years.

"Nicole?"

I blinked and snapped out of my stupor, taking a step back with a short breath. What was I doing? I was falling for Zakari, not getting swept back up in Jerron.

"What, Jerron?" I forced out.

He opened his mouth, then put his hands in his pockets. "I... I needed to see you."

"For what?"

He stared at the ground for a moment, then looked back up at me.

I held his gaze for a millisecond before I had to look away. This was too intense for me.

"Listen, I know you told me not to come to your job again, but Nicole, I feel like I'm going crazy. I can't stop thinking about you. Every day and every night. You have to give me another chance."

"I don't have to do anything!" My heart was beating wildly at his words, but I refused to give him an inkling that I felt any of the same emotions he just described.

He held his hands up. "I know, I'm sorry. I didn't mean to come on too strong, like you owe me something. What I'm trying to say is that I love you, and I miss you. I really hope we can give it another shot. We can sit down and talk about what happened, and I can show you proof that I never betrayed you."

"I found someone new," I blurted before I could stop myself.

He froze. "You what?"

I nodded, trying to convince myself more than him. "I'm back with my high school sweetheart."

Jerron stared at me for a moment, then swallowed. "Nicole, you don't have to pretend to be with someone to hurt me. I understand that you think..."

"I'm not pretending. We've been seeing each other for over a month. His name is Zakari."

"Zakari?"

I nodded again. "Yes. I've moved on, Jerron. You should, too."

He tried again. "Nicole, you don't mean that." He stepped forward, and I stepped back because something told me if I smelled his Calvin Klein cologne I was going to lose it. I held my hands up to stop him from moving any closer, and he halted.

"Please... baby."

I forced back a tear. "I'm not your baby anymore. That's Mario and Shameka."

"We were together for seven years!"

"Shameka had you for even longer than that, and your son needs you."

"Will you at least listen to me?"

The way he said it, the desperation in his tone, made me want to give in, but I couldn't. My mind became filled with doubt, and my heart wanted to believe Jerron was telling the truth, that he hadn't cheated and there was some sort of explanation for all this.

I snapped out of it again, but I was growing weaker by the second. I had to go.

"Jerron, I need to get home."

"Nicole, please."

"Don't come here anymore."

I pushed past him and got in my car.

I refused to look at him as I backed out of my space, but I couldn't help but to peek in my rearview as I exited the parking lot.

Jerron was still standing by his car, watching me as I drove away.

Chapter 36

Zakari

I sucked my teeth, peering at Jerron through my binoculars until he got back into his vehicle to leave Nicole's job.
I knew this day would come.
He couldn't stay away, even if it was for his own good.
What would it take for Jerron to realize I was Nicole's new man? If she hadn't reached out to him since they broke up, that should have been his sign that he was no longer wanted. I surveyed Nicole's call and text logs, as well as her social media records every day. She wasn't thinking anything about Jerron, yet he couldn't let her go.
I didn't like her body language when he approached her. It was like he was weakening her, like she was contemplating giving in to him.
I couldn't have that. Not when Nicole and I were so close to engagement.
It was time to turn up the heat to get Jerron away from her for good. I wasn't sure how I was going to pull that off yet.
Right now, I had to focus on getting some dinner for Nicole. She texted back and forth with Shareese earlier and said she had a taste for Chinese, as well as a bottle of raspberry Stella Rose. I would get the Chinese but not the wine. Couldn't have her getting suspicious like last time.

When I picked out her favorite coffee that Saturday when we went out, she was surprised I knew her order. I had to come up with a quick excuse about remembering it from high school. Thankfully, she didn't remember that I never drank coffee with her in high school. That was a close one, but it wouldn't come that close again.

I couldn't afford it.

I called the restaurant on my way there to place the order.

I had about forty-three minutes to get to Nicole's house at the same time she did. She usually filled up her tank on Tuesdays before she went home. I had to hurry.

I got the order, and thankfully, everything went smoothly.

I studied my tracking system I had on Nicole's car as I drove toward her house from the restaurant. She just arrived. Perfect. She would have just enough time to get comfortable, but not enough to start cooking dinner for herself. Couldn't have my woman wasting food.

I knocked on the door five minutes later with a smile on my face.

Nicole looked surprised to see me. "Zakari? Hey, what are you doing here?"

"Hey!" I beamed, then pulled her in for a hug, proudly holding the bag of food in the other hand.

"What's that?" she asked.

I stared down into her beautiful eyes. "I had a taste for Chinese and thought you might want some, too. I remember we used to eat this all the time back in the day."

Nicole's jaw dropped. "Wow, Zakari! I swear it's like you read my mind. How on earth do you always do this?"

I shot her a mischievous smirk. "Lover's intuition, baby."

A strange look crossed her eyes when I said that, so I backed off. "Let's eat before this gets cold! Unless you're not up for company?"

I stared at her, praying she wouldn't turn me down.

The corners of her lips turned up. "Come on in."

I relaxed as she closed the door behind me, and we made our way to the kitchen.

Nicole and I had an awesome dinner. I had nothing to worry about on Nicole's end when it came to Jerron. Tonight's actions told me that.

Still, he needed a little incentive to stay away.

Chapter 37

Nicole

Things with Zakari were so good they were starting to scare me.

How did he transform from a clingy teenager who couldn't take a hint to a grown man who anticipated my every desire?

I had no idea who taught Zakari how to woo a woman, but I was loving every minute of how he treated me.

I headed to Shareese's house after work on Friday to have a girl's chat. We hadn't done so in a minute, and I was eager to hear about how things were going with her and Vance, especially since he had recently popped the question, and she said yes. I was happy for my friend. She was finally getting what she wanted out of life. It seemed as if things were turning out that way for me, too, as long as things continued to go well with Zakari.

I picked up a couple bottles of wine and some snacks from the store up the street from her house, then headed toward Shareese's apartment.

Excitement filled my heart the closer I got.

We were really doing it, Shareese and me.

Grown women, good jobs, healthy relationships... What more could we ask for?

I knocked on her front door with a smile, but it erased as soon as she opened it.

"What's wrong?" I asked.

"Nothing. My mom is on her way to pick up Benny."

"Hi, Titi!" Benny said as he bounded over to me from the living room floor where he had been playing with his toys.

"Oh, I thought Vance was..." I started, but she held her hand up and shook her head for me to stop.

Just then, we heard a car pull up in the parking lot. Shareese and I looked and saw her mom sliding into the space next to mine.

"Gramma!" Benny shouted and ran to put on his shoes.

Shareese's irritated expression softened as she let out a chuckle.

The boy was working so fast to get out the door, he messed around and put his shoes on the wrong feet.

"Benny, come here!" Shareese said in a fake-exasperated tone as she knelt to help her son switch his shoes around.

"Thank you, Mommy! Bye, Titi!" He grinned up at me and waved before dashing to his grandmother's car, and when I saw Benny's missing front tooth, it stole my heart. I couldn't wait to have babies of my own one day.

Sooner rather than later, hopefully.

"What's up with you?" Shareese asked after she closed the door. She must have noticed my wistful demeanor.

Seeing Benny and his carefree attitude made me think of what I hoped my future with Jerron would look like.

I shook it off. I was with Zakari now, and we could set up our own future, an even better one than I would have thought of with my ex.

"Nothing." I carried the bottles and the bag of snacks to the kitchen. Shareese followed me and grabbed some plates and glasses from her cabinet while I sat everything on the table.

She told Alexa to play some 90s R&B, and the mood immediately shifted.

I took a few sips of wine and ate one of the sandwiches I bought us. I was already feeling better, and judging from the look on Shareese's face, she did, too.

I stared at her, about to ask a question about Vance, when she scrunched up her face, then gasped in laughter.

"What is it?" I said, feeling silly, too.

She got up out of her seat and began singing along with TLC's "What About Your Friends". She told Alexa to turn up the volume. "Remember this?" she asked with a goofy grin, then added a familiar dance move to her singing.

I immediately remembered and joined in. Shareese and I and another girl named Niyah from high school had made a routine to this song back in high school. We won first place, too, because we had gone all out to dress like them. I was T Boz, Shareese was Left Eye, and Niyah was Chili. We really thought we were doing something back then, and I guessed we were because we split a three-hundred-dollar prize that night.

Shareese and I performed the routine to the end, then sat back down full of excitement. "Girl, how did we remember that whole dance?" I asked with a giggle.

She giggled back and rolled her eyes. "No idea, but that was so much fun. I wish Niyah was here. What is she up to nowadays?"

My brows furrowed. "Hm, that's a good question. I lost track of her once we went to college. Let me look at her page."

I looked up Niyah's page, and lo and behold, she had gotten married the day before.

"Wow, this is so cute!" I said, then held out my phone to Shareese so she could see Niyah's wedding photos.

Shareese smiled as she began scrolling, then her expression slowly changed to that of sadness the more she looked at the pictures. She handed the phone back to me when she finished.

"What's wrong?" I asked. "Did something happen?"

She sighed and shook her head. "Nope. What's up with you, though? How are things with Zakari?"

She was deflecting, and I knew it.

"We're good, but I really want to know what's up with you. You can talk to me, Shareese."

She looked down at the table, then back up at me with tears in her eyes. "I think Vance is cheating again."

Just that quickly, the cheerful atmosphere dissipated.

"Are you serious?"

She nodded.

"Why do you think that?"

She shrugged. "Just a hunch. He's being secretive again, hiding his phone, staying out later, all the usual stuff."

She said the words *usual stuff* in such a depressing tone that my heart broke for her. I covered her hand with mine.

"Shareese, I hope he's not, but if he is, you need to leave him, sis. I know you have a child together and have history, but he's not worth the heartache. You're a good woman, and you deserve a man who will treat you like a queen."

Shareese sniffled. "Thank you, Nikki." That was a name she had given me back in high school because she said I was like the sister she had never had. Shareese was the same for me.

I smiled. "No problem, Share Bear."

We stared at each other, then burst out laughing. Neither of us had used those names for each other in ages, but the mere mention of them brought back so many memories.

Nikki and Share Bear. We were two peas in a pod.

I didn't know what the future held for me and Shareese as far as love and relationships, but as long as we stuck together, I knew we'd get through it.

Chapter 38

Zakari

I had to strain a little to hear everything Nicole and Shareese said during their girl's night because of the music, but from what I could glean, I liked Shareese.

I liked her back in high school, too, but people changed, so I needed to know what kind of conversations she and Nicole were having to make sure she wasn't a threat.

Jerron thought he was a threat, but I had something for him.

I wanted to let him off easy, but he forced my hand.

I closed out the app that connected all data from Nicole's phone to my secret one and did a brief search on Shareese's fiancé, Vance.

What was he up to?

Nicole mentioned he proposed, so I thought he and Shareese were happy. I was even planning on having him come to my bachelor's party when me and Nicole got engaged. Lester would be my best man, of course, if he continued to act right, but Vance would definitely be accepted.

I would have to investigate him now, though, to make sure he wouldn't inadvertently ruin anything when it came to my plans with Nicole. If she was busy consoling her best friend over a botched engagement, it might make us push back our wedding date.

"Hold your horses, Zakari!" I chuckled as I forced myself to relax. I hadn't even given Nicole her ring yet, though I had already picked it out.

She had done a few searches online recently through her phone but kept coming back to this one ring with blue diamonds.

I preferred regular diamonds, but if my baby wanted blue, blue would be what she got.

Lester called my phone as I was checking out some photos of the ring and preparing to make my purchase.

I sucked my teeth. "I swear he always calls at the... Hello?" I answered in a neutral tone.

"What's up, man? What are you up to?"

"Nothing, about to call Nicole."

He was silent for a moment. "Okay, cool. I wanted to check in and see if y'all were still coming to play spades with me and Michelle tomorrow?"

I had almost forgotten about the invitation.

"My bad, man. I didn't ask Nicole if she was busy, but I'll ask her as soon as we get off the phone and let you know."

Now that Lester mentioned the spades night, I was glad he called. Getting Nicole acquainted with Michelle was a great idea. Once she and I had a few date nights and game nights with Lester and Michelle, she would see what it would be like to be my wife. Perfect.

"Cool, man, just let me know. Michelle is excited to meet Nicole."

"I sure will! Let me call her now."

"Bet."

I hung up with Lester, and Nicole ended up calling me before I could go to her name in my contacts.

"Hey, Nikki!" I answered with a smile.

"Hi, Zakari... huh?" she responded in a confused tone.

My smile faltered. "What?"

"Did you just call me Nikki?"

I chuckled, though internally I was freaking out. How did I let it slip that I'd heard the name? Now she would know! I had to fix this. "I thought it was a cute name that would fit you is all. Why? You don't like it?"

She was silent for a moment. "It's cool, I guess."

Nicole still sounded leery, so I had to do more damage control. "Anywho, are you busy tomorrow, babe? I meant to ask you earlier, but Lester and Michelle invited us to play spades. Michelle's been dying to meet you."

"Really?" She sounded excited, and I felt myself relax.

"Yup! What do you say?"

"Sure, I'm not busy tomorrow. I'm down. Just tell Lester not to be a sore loser when he and his wife take this loss."

I chuckled. "I'm sure he won't."

Nicole and I chatted for a few more moments about our days, then we called it a night.

I went back on the website to purchase the ring, then closed my laptop.

After watching a few sports highlights, I was ready for bed.

Before I went to sleep, I decided to check Nicole's phone activity to see if anything new came up that I should know about.

My jaw clenched when I saw Jerron had messaged Nicole from a new social media page.

Hey. I know it seems weird to reach out to you from a different profile, but I'm feeling desperate. Nicole, please talk to me.

What do you want, Jerron?

Can we meet tomorrow? Just to talk, I swear.

Nicole didn't write back for ten minutes, so I was about to close out the app. Then my heart stopped when she responded.

Okay, Jerron, but just this once.

Now he had messed up.

Chapter 39

Nicole

Part of me felt like I was betraying Zakari by taking this meeting with Jerron, but another side wanted to see him again.

His face had been etched in my mind ever since he showed up outside my job the other day. Since our breakup, really.

As much as I tried to deny it, I wasn't anywhere near over him.

Zakari and I were moving forward, and things were great, but my heart still longed for Jerron. That infuriated me. Jerron didn't deserve my affections.

Hopefully this meeting would remove those lingering feelings, so I could cut the strings and be free from the prison of attachment to a man who wouldn't do right by me.

Here I was, giving Shareese advice about the type of man she deserved, when I needed to take it myself.

I sat in my car outside the coffee shop, waiting for Jerron to pull up. In between scrolling social media and texting back and forth with Shareese, I looked up every few moments to scan the street in front and behind me to see when he arrived.

Twenty minutes went by before I realized it.

I let out a yawn, then checked the time.

Where are you? I messaged Jerron's new profile.

I pretended to be irritated by him going to such lengths to contact me last night, but in reality, it made my heart skip a beat to see his name across my screen.

According to the activity status in the message thread, Jerron hadn't been online since this morning. I rolled my eyes. Hopefully that didn't mean he was going to be extra late or stand me up. If he did, I swore...

A call buzzed in from Tina. I wrinkled my nose. "What does she want?" Not that I had a problem with her, but I figured I wouldn't hear from Tina again since I told her in no uncertain terms, I wanted nothing else to do with Jerron.

Did he tell her we were meeting today? "Hello?" I answered.

"Hi, Nicole..." Tina's voice wavered as she spoke, and it made me sit alert. Did something happen to Mike? Oh no! I felt like a total jerk for being upset that she reached out to me now. Tina had told me before that she didn't have too many girlfriends, but she had immediately clicked with me. My heart sank as I swallowed and prepared to hear the bad news.

"Hey, Tina... What's going on?"

"There... there was an accident!" She choked up.

"Oh no, I'm so sorry! Where are you? Is Mike in the hospital?"

"It's not Mike, it's Jerron."

I almost dropped the phone. "Jerron? Where is he?" I felt my blood pressure raising as reality hit me. That was why Jerron was late. Something happened to him.

"He's at Westin Hospital. Me and Mike are on our way. I wanted to let you know because he told us last night he was going to meet you today."

My ears burned at that news. If Jerron told Tina and Mike we were meeting, he must have had a genuine reason for reaching out to me. Why tell them if he didn't?

"I'm on my way!"

I raced to the hospital, not sure what I would find when I got there. I was so scared.

"Lord, please let him be okay," I prayed repeatedly. Jerron and I might have had our issues, but I would never wish harm on him.

I spotted Mike and Tina off to the side of me as I power-walked across the parking lot. I slowed my pace so they could catch up. Both looked frazzled, like they had been in the middle of something when they got the call.

Tina addressed me first, her baby bump more evident than it was the last time we saw each other. That increased my guilt. "Jerron's mother told us he was here."

I nodded, and we all entered the Emergency Room entrance, but when we got inside, Mike stopped short.

Tina and I looked back at him.

"Let's pray," he said. We grabbed each other's hands, and Mike said a quick prayer for Jerron. My heart beat with every word.

When we opened our eyes, it was time to see how bad it was.

When we got to the ICU, thankfully, there was good news. Jerron's mother greeted us with a grim expression on her face. "Thank you for coming," she said.

She stared at me, and I felt awkward, but now wasn't the time to express it.

"How is he?" I asked, afraid to hear the answer.

She sighed. "They're working on him. Thankfully, it doesn't look like there will be any brain damage, but he did break several bones in one of his arms and legs."

"How did the accident happen?" Mike asked.

Jerron's mother sighed again. "Jerron was crossing through an intersection, and a car ran a red light and crashed right into him. The other guy fled the scene. He was driving one of those huge trucks, but it had no plates on it. My baby could have died."

Her lip quivered when she said those last words, and I reached up to rub her back.

The doctors wouldn't let us see Jerron, so his mother told us to come back the next day. I was definitely coming back to visit, and I prayed Jerron would have a full recovery from his injuries.

Chapter 40

Zakari

Sometimes you had to get your hands a little dirty to make the pathway clean.

I submitted Keno's payment on the app as promised, then the transaction was completed. Hopefully we wouldn't be hearing from the likes of Jerron any time soon, and even if we did, Nicole and I would already be married.

I was at the mall picking up Nicole's ring from the jewelry store. The Lord worked it out that the same day Jerron was removed from the equation, they called me to say it had come in. I inspected the ring as the jeweler watched, and it was even more beautiful up close than it was on the website.

"It's perfect!" I said, and the jeweler smiled with me. I completed the transaction and exited the store, whistling along the way.

"Zakari?" a familiar female voice sounded to the left of me. I turned. It was Shareese. I didn't feel like being bothered, especially since I planned to start writing my proposal speech as soon as I got home, but I supposed I could entertain some foolishness for a few moments.

"Hey, Shareese!" I forced a smile.

"Hey. What are you up to?" she asked. She peered at the jewelry store, then back at me.

"Shopping," I replied in a flat tone.

She gave me a look. "...Okay. Have you talked to Nicole today?"

"Not yet. I planned to call her on my way home." I hoped she caught the hint.

"Okay, well if you speak to her before I do, please tell her to call me."

"Yup." I resumed my trek back to the parking lot.

"Zakari?"

I tensed and turned back. "Yes?"

She stared at me for a long moment. "Nothing."

I rolled my eyes when I faced the opposite direction and quickly exited the mall.

Shareese

There was something weird about Zakari.

It wasn't necessarily anything he said, but his body language seemed off to me. I couldn't put my finger on why, though. He was rude to me, like he wanted to rush to leave the conversation, when all I said was hi.

Then the fact that he was coming out of a jewelry store with a bag in his hand... Zakari and Nicole had barely dated three months.

I hoped he wasn't planning to propose to her.

Not that I was a hater, but I knew my friend wasn't over Jerron. It was in her voice whenever she spoke about him, not to mention she was clearly forcing it whenever she bragged about the latest thing Zakari did.

I remembered how back in high school Nicole always complained about Zakari and was desperate to leave him. What changed?

Nothing much from my stance, except she was on the rebound this time.

I hoped her misguided attempt to get back at Jerron wouldn't have her doing anything stupid. If so, I would definitely have to say something.

Chapter 41

Nicole

I clutched the flowers as my heels clicked down the hospital hallway. Jerron had been moved to a regular room this morning, and they were now allowing him to see visitors. I was so nervous. I had no idea what I would say to him.

Hearing about the accident had my mind swimming. I accidentally called Zakari by Jerron's name three times last night as we spoke on the phone, then I broke down and told him about the accident.

He seemed to understand because he immediately jumped in to comfort me instead of getting upset.

"Nicole, don't worry. Your friend is going to be okay." He didn't have a problem with me coming to visit Jerron at the hospital today, either. That was mature of him. I would think that a man would freak out about their woman going to see about another man. Not Zakari. He constantly amazed me with how understanding and solid he was.

I took a deep breath as I turned the corner that led to Jerron's room, mentally rehearsing my speech I was sure I would forget every word of as soon as I saw him.

Unfortunately, my speech was not necessary.

Jerron was already being taken care of.

By Shameka.

She stopped short when she saw me as she exited the room. "Nicole?" she gasped. "What are you doing here?"

It all came back to me. Jerron's mother had stared at me for a few moments yesterday when I came with Mike and Tina. I thought it was because she was surprised I came. Now I knew the real reason.

"I... I heard about the accident." I swallowed as I tried to gather my bearings. Shameka's presence caught me completely off guard.

"Did Momma Lena tell you to stop by?"

"Momma Lena?" I couldn't help but repeat it to make sure I heard her correctly. Jerron's mother's name was Valena, but she always told me to call her Mrs. Davis.

Clearly, she and Shameka had longevity.

I felt my cheeks growing hot with embarrassment. "I'll just leave these with him," I mustered.

Shameka nodded and gestured toward the room like she was unbothered by my presence, even grateful that I stopped by. "Sure! Go on in. He just fell asleep, though."

I drew in a breath and walked by her as she traveled toward the exit. When I walked into Jerron's room, the dagger in my heart twisted.

He was laying there asleep, as Shameka said, and his left arm and leg were propped up and covered in bandages. It broke my heart, and I burst into tears, covering my face with my hand. I set the flowers down on the gift table with my other hand, then fanned my face to compose myself.

I crept closer to Jerron because I didn't want to wake him, but when I got next to him, I wished I didn't.

There were kiss marks on his cheek and forehead, the same color as the lipstick Shameka was wearing.

Chapter 42

Zakari

Everything was going according to plan. I would give Nicole a few days to get over Jerron's accident, then I would make my move.

I would be the perfect gentleman.

From what she was telling Shareese, everything I was doing was having the desired effect. Shareese didn't seem too thrilled about me, though. I would have to keep an eye on her. If she tried anything to ruin what we were building, I had something for her.

In other news, Nicole and I had our third spades night with Lester and Michelle last night. We had a blast.

Of course, Nicole and I won, but it was because we got so good at guessing each other's hands with various facial expressions. Lester jokingly accused us of cheating, but we all laughed it off since they had beaten us the first time we played.

The pinnacle of the night came when Michelle brought Jerron up. At first, I thought things were going to take a negative turn, but it worked out in my favor.

"Nicole, I am so sorry to hear about what happened to your friend," Michelle had said.

Nicole's expression changed when she said that, so I covered her hand with mine.

"Thank you," she said, then she looked at me. "Zakari has been a true support."

I smiled, and Michelle gave me an approving look.

"Zakari, you are so sweet!" She turned to Lester. "Somebody needs to take notes!" We shared another laugh at that, then the jovial mood continued.

By the end of the night, it seemed we had another one in the books.

I stared at Nicole's engagement ring for a few seconds, then closed the box and put it back in its bag.

Nicole was supposed to come visit my house for the first time next weekend. Soon to be our home. She was gonna freak out when she saw how big it was. I purposefully downplayed its size just for that reason, and I also made sure we always ended up hanging out at her house before finally inviting her over for dinner.

I perfected my steak and mashed potatoes recipe. Nicole liked her steak medium well, and it took me seven attempts to figure it out, but I had done it. She was in for a treat.

Lester called my phone, interrupting my thought process as usual. "Hello?" This time I didn't answer in an irritable tone because nothing was in my way anymore. Nicole was mine.

"Hey, Zakari... you got a minute?"

The way he asked the question gave me pause, but I bit the bait. "What's up?"

I heard the sound of his blinker turning on. He must have been driving home. "Is everything okay with you?"

"Yeah... why?"

"Because I noticed at dinner last night when Michelle mentioned Jerron, you sort of tensed up."

"Tensed up?" I repeated as if I was clueless as to what he was referring to.

"Yeah, man. Are you and Nicole having problems?"

"Having problems? Why would you think that? You heard Nicole tell Michelle I've been a great help." I felt myself getting tense, so I took a breath to regain my composure.

"No need to fly off the handle. It was just a question."

That was it. It had been a long time coming, but Lester was about to hear a piece of my mind. "You know what, Lester? You always had a problem with me and Nicole's relationship, even back when we were in high school. Why you always hatin', man?"

"I'm not hating, Zakari. I'm just trying to make sure you're not getting played and that she's being for real this time."

"Being for real... What are you talking about? You think Nicole doesn't feel the same way for me that I feel for her? Why is she with me then?"

"Again, calm down. I'm not trying to hate on your relationship. I want to see you happy, but I want it to be with a woman that is right for you."

"Nicole is right for me."

"Zakari... Never mind."

"No, go ahead and say it."

"It's nothing, man. Sorry I bothered you."

"You're good."

We talked about other things after that, but Lester's comments had gotten under my skin. Nicole and I were so close. No one was getting in the way of that. Looked like I was going to have to keep an eye on my best friend, too.

Chapter 43

Nicole

Shareese and I were having another girl's night at her apartment. I was supposed to go visit Zakari's house for the first time tomorrow.

We were having a few drinks while we ate pizza and watched *Housewife* shows, then we planned to make sundaes to top the night off.

"Girl, I always have the best time with you," I said.

Shareese took a sip of her drink and nodded. "Same here."

I sat my drink down on the coffee table. We were sitting in her living room with the big screen. She had a smaller screen in her kitchen and a mid-sized one in her bedroom.

"How are things with Vance?"

The mood immediately shifted. Shareese stopped mid-movement as she was reaching for another slice of pizza.

"Now why'd you have to ask that? I was trying not to think of him tonight or what he could be out there doing."

"Where is he?"

She used her fingers for air quotes. "Working late."

I sighed. "Shareese, you're going to have to confront him sooner or later."

She stared at a stray strand of cheese that had gotten onto the coffee table next to the pizza box. "I know."

Then she shrugged as if to shake it off before turning back to face me. "How are things with Zakari?"

The way she said his name made me question why she asked that. "We're good, why?"

"Hm."

I picked up on something once again in the way she said that. "Hm, what?"

Shareese reached for her drink again. "Be careful with that one, that's all I'm saying."

"What do you mean, be careful with that one?"

"He's weird."

I didn't know if it was the alcohol I'd consumed, or the tone she was using as she spoke to me, but Shareese was pissing me off.

"I think you need to worry about your man's erratic behavior instead of mine."

She cocked her head like she was surprised I went there, but she took it there first, so I was game for whatever came out of her mouth next.

"Listen, Nicole, I'm just trying to be your friend here."

"And so am I."

We held each other's gazes for a few moments, then let it go and continued eating pizza and watching the shows. By the end of the night, we were back to normal, but I couldn't help but wonder what Shareese was getting at.

First, she didn't like Jerron, and now, she didn't like Zakari? What was her deal?

Chapter 44

Zakari

It was time for Shareese to be taken out of the picture. I didn't want to move too quickly, since Nicole seemed to just be getting over Jerron's accident, but just like Jerron, Shareese was forcing my hand.

Lucky for her, her simple little boyfriend, Vance, wasn't cheating on her, but certain arrangements could be made to make it appear that way. All Shareese had to do was say one more thing. Rasheeda was on speed dial.

I made lots of friends in college. Well, not necessarily friends. More like associates. Ones who would fly down in a heartbeat to make a quick buck, then be back on their way out of town. Shareese would be none the wiser, and her little marriage-and-family fantasy of things finally going right with Vance could go up in flames.

Nicole had finally seen our house, and she loved it.

"Zakari, wow, this is beautiful!" I watched as her eyes took in the three acres of land that our eight-bedroom mini-mansion was located on.

I took her on a tour of our fully furnished home, taking note of the fact that she liked the way I decorated things. I always had good taste, even since high school. I should have gone into interior design and fashion rather than mechanical engineering.

Nicole loved it all the same, though.

She gushed at the jacuzzi in our basement, and I could not wait until she was my wife so we could spend lustful nights there together.

Just seeing her in the room with the jacuzzi made me want to forget what I had planned and propose right there.

I held myself back because the proposal was coming later that day.

I had it perfectly set up. She would go into our dining room last and see the little blue box sitting on the coffee table, its color matching perfectly with the blue and beige decor of the couches, paintings, and walls.

"Zakari, what is this?" she asked with a gasp, staring at the box, then walking over to it. I knelt as she picked up the ring box and opened it, seeing her ring for the first time.

She turned back to see me in position. "What are you..." She stared back and forth between the twinkle in my eyes and the ring she was holding.

I cleared my throat. "Nicole, I don't know if you remember this, but one night we went to a revival at my church. There was a man of God there named Prophet Lincoln. Do you remember what he said to us?"

Nicole froze as if she remembered. "He said I was going to be your wife."

I smiled. She remembered, like I knew she would. "He did, baby, and I've been wanting to do this for a while, but tonight I want to make it official. I feel like we ran into each other again all these years later for a reason. It just so happened that we were both single and ready to make such a great commitment. You make me happy, and I would love to make you happy for the rest of your life. Will you be my wife?"

The tears in her eyes confirmed what I knew she would say before she said it.

"Yes!" she gushed, and I stood to gently take the ring box from her delicate hand and slide the ring on her finger.

It fit perfectly.

Look at God.

Chapter 45

Nicole

This was magical.

It was the second time I'd been engaged, but this time, I believed it was going to happen. Since Shareese seemed to have reservations about me and Zakari, I decided to go to my mom's house first to tell her.

I figured her congratulations would help soften the blow if Shareese said anything out of pocket. "Hey, Momma!" I said in a silly voice as I entered her house with my key. I couldn't wait until my mom saw Zakari's house. It was huge.

Who knew he was sitting on three acres? He was always so humble, and he smiled bashfully the first time we talked, and he told me he owned his home. I was thinking it would be a starter house or a fixer upper, but no. Zakari did it big, and from the way everything looked, he was doing a great job of maintaining it.

I was proud of him.

My mother rested her hand on her left hip. "What brings you here?"

I lowered my tone as I gave her a gleeful gaze. "I have news..."

She looked me up and down. "What news? You better not be pregnant."

"Mom!"

"What? You're of age. I ain't foolish enough to think you're still a virgin."

That stung a little, but I guessed it made sense with the way society operated nowadays. I sighed. "I'm not pregnant, Mom, but I am engaged."

She raised her brows in surprise. "To Zakari?"

I nodded.

"Wow."

I didn't like the fact that she was acting all mystified, but I pressed forward to tell her how he did it.

"... And then, he mentioned that night we went to the revival that summer. There was a prophet there, and he..."

"Every voice ain't from God," she said, cutting me off.

"Huh?"

"Every voice ain't from God," she repeated as if that would make it make any more sense.

"I'm not following."

She shrugged. "You'll figure it out sooner or later. How's Jerron doing?"

I stared at her. Why was everyone being so rude lately? "I don't know. You'll have to ask his baby's mother."

My mother rolled her eyes. I wasn't going to bother to ask her what that was about.

"What did Shareese say when you told her you got engaged?"

"I haven't told her yet."

"Oh really? Why not?" The way she asked the question was like she was feigning surprise, like she already knew I didn't tell Shareese and why I hadn't done so.

"I was going to tell her after I told you. Since you're the mother of the bride."

My shoulders slumped, and my eyes filled with tears. Why couldn't anyone be happy for me?

My mom's expression softened when she saw my demeanor change.

"Congratulations, Nicole. I hope everything works out for you."

I suddenly wanted to leave. "Thanks," I responded, but it wasn't sincere, just like her congratulations.

Chapter 46

Zakari

I would let Nicole plan the wedding since I'd done everything else. I could not wait to see what she came up with.

I called Lester for a change, as I was driving home from work. "Hello?" he answered on the third ring, giving me the same irritable tone I often gave him when he called.

"Hey, what's up with you?" I greeted him with a smile in my voice.

"Nothing, Michelle's just getting on my nerves."

"Oh, trouble in paradise?" I joked.

He sighed. "Yeah, she keeps on nagging, man."

"Nagging about what?"

"Asking me to do things around the house, then getting mad when I don't do it immediately."

"Oh..." I was already losing interest in this conversation, especially since it wasn't the reason I called.

"Anyway, what's up with you?"

I straightened up and cleared my throat, drawing out my words as I spoke. "I proposed to Nicole the other day..."

"... And?"

"She said yes!"

Silence. Go figure. "Congratulations, man," he said like that was the last thing he was truly feeling.

Still, I kept my tone lighthearted. "You gonna be my best man?"

He sighed. "Yes, Zakari."

"What's wrong?"

"Nothing."

"... Okay."

"Actually, are you sure that's the right decision, man?"

"Of course, it's the right decision. Why do you keep asking me that?"

"Because to be completely honest, it doesn't seem like Nicole is that into you."

"Yet she just accepted my proposal for engagement."

"As long as you're happy."

"I am."

"Then I'm happy for you."

After we hung up, my mind was stewing. What right did Lester have to question my decisions? I never questioned anything he did, even when we were in college, and he was hoeing around. Lester slept with so many women, it was a wonder he never caught an STD. And he was worried about me making the right decision?

He needed to look in a mirror.

Lester's attitude toward me and Nicole's relationship was starting to make me question his loyalty. Not that I thought he would try anything with Nicole, but he might do something to sabotage our bond.

I couldn't have that.

Chapter 47

Nicole

I pulled up to Shareese's apartment contemplating whether I wanted to go in. My mom's less than jovial response to me and Zakari's engagement was making me think we might as well elope.

Hopefully his parents would have a better reaction.

I sighed and opened my driver's side door just as Shareese was exiting her front door.

"Hey!" She looked like she was surprised to see me.

"Hey." I got out of my car, and we shared a hug.

"What brings you here?" she asked, and it gave me deja vu. My mom had asked the same question before she bashed me and Zakari's engagement.

I chose my words carefully. "I have some news." My heart fluttered. I hoped my best friend would come through with the congratulations and encouragement I needed.

"I have some news too, actually," she said, and there was a hint of a smile behind her eyes.

"What's your news?" I asked.

Her face flushed then scrunched as if she was about to let out an ugly cry. She took a deep breath and fanned her face. "Nicole, Vance wasn't cheating."

My jaw dropped in shock. "He wasn't?"

She shook her head. "No. He really was working all those late hours. He picked up a second job, which was why when I called his first job to confirm he was on the road, they didn't know what I was talking about."

I held my hand up. "Wait, you called his job to confirm he was working? When did this happen? You didn't tell me you planned to investigate."

She shook her head. "I know, I know. I just wanted to find out myself first so I could process it because Nicole, if he was doing it again, it was really over this time. I had already started the application for child support and everything."

Wow. Shareese was definitely serious if she had done all that.

She continued. "It turns out, he picked up a second job, like I said earlier. I found that out when I followed him to work one night."

My eyes widened. "You did what?"

She nodded. "Yup. I was pissed. I thought he was lying to me, so I wanted to catch him in the act like I accidentally did the first time he cheated. I stayed a few cars behind the whole time while he drove to this bar. I planned to lay into him as soon as I walked up on him and whatever chick he was messing with. Then I got the shock of my life when I went inside half an hour later, and he was behind the counter."

"Behind the counter?"

"He got his bartender's license, and he was using the extra money to surprise me with a honeymoon after our wedding." Her lower lip quivered. "Nicole... it was so sweet. He spotted me when I was about to leave and had his friend cover for him. We talked, and that's when he explained everything."

"Wow." This was great news.

Shareese sniffled, and I grabbed a tissue from my purse to give to her. "I am so happy for you, sis. I know this is what you wanted."

Seeing my friend in tears over her man finally doing right by her made me want to start bawling myself. Why hadn't Jerron done the same for me?

That didn't matter, though. It was all about me and Zakari now.

Chapter 48

Nicole

I went to work the next day feeling elated. Things were finally going right. I was getting married to Zakari, and Shareese and Vance's relationship was in a good place.

All the pain we had both gone through because of our relationships was turning around in our favor. I listened to Tye Tribbet's "He Turned It" on the way to the hospital.

When I walked inside, one of the higher-level managers, Clarissa, pulled me aside.

"Nicole, good. You're here early. Follow me, please."

She began walking down the hallway, and I froze for a second before following her. What was this about? I racked my brains trying to think. I didn't have any training sessions scheduled today. I had submitted all my reports on Friday. What was Clarissa's deal? Why was her facial expression so serious?

She turned the corner leading to the Human Resources office.

My heart dropped. Why was she bringing me to HR?

When she stopped in front of the door, then opened it to usher me inside, I snapped out of it. "Clarissa, what is this about?"

Her face still held its grim expression. "Come on in, and we'll discuss it once we sit down."

I blinked and tried to read her, but I wasn't getting anything. The feeling in the pit of my stomach grew though. This wasn't going to be good, whatever it was.

I entered the room to see another one of the upper-level managers and the Human Resource manager. They gestured for me to sit at the small rectangular table with them, so I did, and Clarissa sat on their side of the table across from me.

I opened my mouth to ask what was going on, when Ashley, the Human Resource manager, cut in.

"Hello, Nicole. I hope you've had a great morning."

"I have... How are you? Why am I here this morning if I may ask?"

Neither of the other managers said anything.

Ashley's lips formed a straight line. "Nicole, unfortunately, due to a recent set of circumstances, we're going to have to terminate our relationship with you, effective immediately."

I sputtered in response. "Terminate our relationship... I'm fired?" My eyes shot to Clarissa, but she was staring down at the table. The other upper-level manager, Carlos, was staring at the point beyond my left shoulder. This was bizarre. I focused on Ashley.

"Ashley, may I ask why I'm being fired?"

She sighed. "It looks like your reports from the past few months have had inaccurate numbers. The numbers you provided made it appear that the supervisors you were overseeing were doing better than they actually were when it came to hospital protocols. As you know, providing inaccurate data like this causes the hospital to lose credibility, especially if something were to go wrong with a patient's care."

I could not believe this. "Ashley, none of my reports were lies. I follow the practice of evaluating my employees and giving them a chance to make changes before submitting the final reports. You know this, and my process was approved. I don't understand what's going on here."

I stared at all three of them, but the only one who was looking back at me was Ashley. Something was up with this. Why was I really being fired? What weren't they telling me?

Ashley continued as if I hadn't said anything. "We value the time you spent here and the work you've done to improve the various assignments you've overseen. Because of this, we won't put any of this information on your employee record, so it won't hurt your chances of gaining employment elsewhere."

I came out of character for a second. "Are you freaking serious? Don't play with me, Ashley. You aren't withholding information from my record to help me get a better job. You're doing that because it's not true that I did the things you're accusing me of. What is really going on here?"

Carlos and Clarissa were still refusing to look at me.

I stood and pushed my chair into the table. "None of you want to tell me the real reason I'm being fired? Fine, you will be hearing from my attorney."

I stalked out of the room, and none of them tried to stop me.

My eyes blurred with tears as I made my way to my car. I was numb with disbelief. They really fired me? Was I not dreaming?

I sat in my car trying to figure out what could be happening behind the scenes. I couldn't come up with anything. I was a stellar employee since the day I started. I followed all protocols and treated everyone fairly, while other managers cut corners and only bothered to do what was right when the whole hospital was under evaluation.

Where had I gone wrong?

Chapter 49

Zakari

Nicole sounded so distraught over the phone when she told me she lost her job, I knew I had to see her immediately. I took my lunch break and headed to her apartment.

She let me in, then plopped on the couch with a dazed expression on her face.

"What happened?" I asked, sitting next to her and putting my arm around her shoulders.

"Zakari, I have no idea. I went in there expecting business as usual and walked out without a job."

I listened as she continued the story, telling me every detail of what her managers had done to her. My heart hurt to see her hurt. Nicole was a good woman. She deserved better than this.

"Nicole, I am so sorry to hear this happened to you. If you want to move forward with the lawsuit, you know I'll do anything I can to help."

She shook her head, then plopped her face into her hands. "I can't even think about a lawsuit right now, Zakari. We were supposed to get married. Now I have to figure out how I'm going to pay my rent, much less everything else for the wedding."

"I'll fund the wedding."

She looked at me. "No, I can't let you do that."

"Why not? It's both of our money, anyway, and besides, I'm the man. I can handle it, Nicole."

Her expression softened for a second. "What about my apartment, though? I have to stay afloat, and I don't want to dip into my savings because of this. I guess I have to, but this just sucks. It totally blindsided me. I need to start filling out applications, but that might mess us up if I get something quickly, because we were supposed to get married in three months. What if I can't get the time off from my new job?"

I did my best to ease her fears. "Nicole, don't worry about all that. How about this… you can end your lease and move in with me. That way you won't have to worry about scrambling to find another job immediately. You can start looking after we get married. Heck, we can even push the date up if that makes you more comfortable."

She stared at me. "I don't know, Zakari. I don't want to impose on you…"

I waved off her concern with a flip of the wrist. "Impose on me? Are you kidding? Nicole, you are about to be my wife. I would do anything for you. Plus, you were going to move in anyway. It will just be a little earlier than we thought. Why don't we talk to your landlord now and see about getting your things moved to my place?"

She was giving in, I could tell.

"But what about… I really didn't want to officially move in before we get married. I don't want to mess around and fall into temptation."

Again, I assuaged her anxieties. "We can sleep in separate rooms. Or why don't you move your big stuff to my place, then take your essentials to your mom's house? I'm sure she wouldn't mind letting you stay there 'til we tie the knot."

She shook her head at that suggestion, like I knew she would.

"No, I don't want to move in with my mom, and Shareese is about to get married herself, so that's out of the question. I guess it makes the most sense for me to move in with you."

I relaxed, then pulled her closer, kissing the top of her head. "We'll be fine, babe. I make enough to take care of both of us until you get your new job. Don't worry about expenses. We can sort all that out after the wedding. That way you can hold onto your savings. I know you worked hard to build it."

Tears of relief filled her eyes. "Thank you so much, Zakari. I'm so glad to have you in my life."

"Same here, babe. I would do anything for you."

Chapter 50

Nicole

Zakari was literally the perfect man.

We went to my landlord's office together, and at first, she wasn't going to let me out of my lease without paying the remaining month's rent, but Zakari stepped in like a knight in shining armor. He wooed the landlord, laying the charm on thick and explaining how we were about to get married soon, so I would be leaving anyway. In the end, she agreed to let me out of the lease when Zakari offered to pay her a thousand dollars via a cashier's check and find a new tenant to take my place immediately.

I had no idea he had such a way with words.

"How are we going to find a new tenant that quickly?" I asked when we exited the office.

Zakari turned to me with a smile. "Have no worries, babe. I already know someone who's looking."

My jaw dropped. "You do? Who?"

"One of my old friends from college. They just relocated to the area and are staying with roommates. I'll let them know I found them a nice spot, and they'll jump at the opportunity to move in."

I stared at him in awe. "Wow, Zakari. You got all types of connections!"

He grinned. "Anything for my baby!"

Zakari called his friend on Bluetooth, and just like he said, his friend, Rasheeda, jumped at the opportunity.

My things were moved the next day, or what I kept of it, at least. I left my furniture to Rasheeda as a way of saying thanks for taking over my former responsibility and moved all my essentials to Zakari's house. Our house now, I guessed.

I took a bedroom on the opposite end of the hallway from Zakari. Hopefully that would help us not to fall into temptation because the way he swooped in and saved the day had me feeling all types of emotions.

I was living a real-life fairytale.

I finished rearranging my room to my liking, then traveled downstairs. I planned to cook a nice dinner as a thanks to Zakari for all he had done, but he beat me to it.

"Hey, babe!" he said, giving me a kiss as he stirred the pot of rice, then replaced the lid.

I had no idea why the smell of fried chicken didn't hit me upstairs in my room, but my mouth was watering now, nonetheless.

"This looks great! Thank you for cooking."

Zakari shrugged like it was no big deal. "Of course, woman! I knew you would be tired from getting your room together. Did everything fit how you wanted it?"

I nodded. "Sure did. Not like I'll be staying there long, anyway." Zakari and I decided to move our wedding date up to next month.

Everything was happening so quickly, I barely had time to breathe.

Zakari finished cooking and started fixing our plates, so I ran to one of the bathrooms to wash my hands.

When I returned to the table, my place was already set and equipped with a plate and utensils.

"What do you want to drink?" Zakari asked with his head in the refrigerator.

"Soda is fine," I said, knowing it was probably a bad idea since I was trying to keep my weight down in preparation for our special day.

"Soda it is!" He chuckled, and I watched him pour us both a glass, then bring them to the table.

"Thank you," I said when he handed mine to me.

"I'm so glad you're here." Zakari took a sip.

"Me too." I raised my glass, and we clinked them together before sharing our meal.

I planned to start submitting applications to new jobs the next morning, but when I woke up, I was so tired that I decided to rest instead. The events of the previous day must have taken more out of me than I originally thought.

"Oh well. Plenty of time for that later," I reasoned.

Chapter 51

Zakari

Everything was going according to plan. Before I knew it, Nicole would be my wife. It was a dream come true to know she was right down the hall from where I slept and that I would soon be waking up and staring into her beautiful eyes every morning.

I zipped through my shift at work, then returned home to spend the evening with my future bride.

When I entered our living room, Nicole looked frustrated.

"What's wrong?" I asked, carrying my suitcase to my office, and then re-entering the living room to join her.

She rolled her eyes. "First off, my laptop just died, like out of nowhere. I have no idea what happened. It was working fine a couple days ago, then when I sat down to fill out some applications for a new job, it wouldn't turn on."

"Wow, that sucks. I know it's a pain, but you can feel free to use the desktop in my office for your applications." I pointed toward the office for emphasis.

She was silent for a second. "Thanks, Zakari. I didn't even think to ask."

I smiled. "It's no worry, babe. You're probably just getting used to the idea of us sharing our household. It's strange to me, too, but I love it."

She smiled back. "Me too. Thanks."

"Is there anything else bothering you?" I braced myself for her answer.

She sighed. "Yup. It appears Shareese isn't too thrilled about us moving up our wedding date."

"She's not?" I feigned surprise.

Nicole shook her head. "Nope. When I told her today, she practically bit my head off. She's becoming so selfish since it's official that her and Vance are getting married. I suggested a double wedding, and she looked at me like I was crazy."

I raised a brow, then nodded in understanding. "You know, Nicole, I think Shareese is jealous of you."

She cocked her head at me. "Jealous? Why do you say that?"

I chose my next words carefully. "Just little things. I don't want to get into the whole story, but what I will say is that she probably knows that our wedding was going to be bigger than hers, and then there's the fact that her and Vance had so many issues before he finally decided to stop messing around on her, and then..." I looked away. "Never mind."

She was hanging on my every word. "Never mind what?"

"I don't want to get into it."

She sat up in her seat. "Get into what, Zakari?"

I held my hand up. "No, that's your best friend. I'm not getting in between anything."

Nicole stood. "No, Zakari, whatever it is, it sounds like I need to know. I have never taken Shareese as a jealous person, so I don't think she is, but if there is something I need to know, you need to tell me."

I took a few moments before giving in. "Listen, I don't want to cause any trouble. It's just... a couple of weeks after we started getting reacquainted with each other, Shareese reached out to me."

Nicole's eyes narrowed, and she crossed her arms. "And said what?"

I swallowed. "It's probably best if I showed you."

I scrolled through my phone until I found the screenshots, then handed my phone to Nicole. She scrolled through them, page after page, until she looked back up at me with tears in her eyes. "I can't believe this!"

I shook my head. "Me neither, babe. I thought she was just reaching out as a friend at first, you know, because we had just started talking, but then when she started talking about how things were going badly with Vance, I got confused."

Nicole sniffled. "She really tried to get with you, and the whole time she was..."

It was my turn to be upset. "The whole time she was what?"

Nicole shook her head. "It doesn't matter. I can't believe she was calling herself my best friend the whole time you and I were seeing each other, but behind my back, she was trying to get with you."

I walked over and wrapped my arms around her. "Nicole, I didn't mean to upset you, especially with everything you're already going through, but honestly, what happened with Shareese has been weighing on my chest. It didn't feel right not to tell you."

"I appreciate you." She looked up at me, and I leaned down to kiss her softly.

"No doubt. And just so you know, I blocked her after she sent that last message about us meeting up somewhere."

Nicole grimaced as if what I had just said disgusted her. Then a faraway look crossed her eyes. "I should have known she was capable of something like this. You know she came out and told me a while back that her and Jerron dated before we got together?"

My jaw dropped. "She did?"

Nicole nodded. "I wasn't going to take it to heart because she said it happened before me and Jerron got together, and she told me they never slept with each other. Now I know that was a lie. I feel so stupid." Her eyes clouded again, and I held her tighter.

"Hey. Don't beat yourself up. If it makes you feel any better, Lester has been against our relationship since day one."

Nicole's jaw dropped. "Lester? For real?"

I nodded and gave her a look like I was hurt. "He seems to be coming around to the idea now that Michelle is on board, but it sucks that it took his wife to convince him to be happy for me, and not the fact that I was his best friend."

Nicole shook her head. "Wow. Well, at least we have each other, right?"

I smiled. "You're right about that. Always."

I leaned down to give her a deeper kiss.

Chapter 52

Nicole

As quickly as it seemed my life was coming together, now it was falling back apart. I didn't have the strength to go toe to toe about what Shareese said to Zakari in those messages, so I decided to let it go until after Zakari and I got married.

I would still go to Shareese's wedding and serve as her maid of honor, but I wouldn't bother to include her in mine.

Zakari and I would likely go to the courthouse instead of having a formal ceremony, since neither of us had great support for our union.

I wouldn't even tell Shareese our plans until after it was done. Then I would confront her about what she tried to do with my man behind my back and about the fact that she lied to me about not sleeping with Jerron.

I was depressed.

For the past three days, it had been hard to get out of bed in the morning. I didn't have the energy to fill out applications or do much but lay in bed and watch TV.

I knew I would snap out of it sooner or later, but for now, I would allow myself to wallow as I awaited our wedding.

That feeling lasted a day.

I wasn't going to sit there and do nothing for almost a month. I dusted my shoulders off and went to Zakari's office to fill out some applications. I filled out two at a nearby hospital, then a third one in another city. By the time I finished, I was proud of myself.

Things were going to come back together for me. I just had to be patient.

Shareese

Nicole had been dodging my phone calls lately, which was weird. I was trying to reach her to tell her I was sorry about getting upset when she mentioned us having a double wedding.

It wasn't that I thought it was a bad idea, it was that she caught me off guard. Plus, I was hormonal because I was pregnant again.

I hadn't told Nicole about the new baby because Vance and I were waiting until I was further along to share the news with everyone.

I headed to the mall to pick out some decorative items I planned to put together as centerpieces for our wedding. It wasn't going to be big, maybe fifty people at the most between both of our families, but still, I wanted the banquet hall to look like a million bucks. Vance and I weren't rich by any means, but that didn't mean we couldn't have class. I browsed countless aisles of the store, finding a bunch of great pieces I could coordinate to make the tables pop. By the time I finished, I was pleased with my selections.

I exited the store, carrying the heavy bag. I knew I shouldn't be carrying it myself, but Vance was at work, and Nicole wasn't answering her phone.

My car wasn't parked far from the entrance anyway.

I was almost near the exit when I saw a familiar-faced female enter through the same door I was going out. I stepped aside to let her and the little girl who was holding her hand to go through, then it dawned on me who she was.

"Shameka?"

She turned back and looked me up and down, likely trying to figure out who I was. "Yes? Do I know you from somewhere?"

I shook my head and mustered a quick reply. "No, we're just social media friends." It was true, because I had joined some groups she was in and sent her a friend request while I was trying to find information for Nicole.

She nodded in understanding, then gave me a wave before resuming her walk. "Nice to see you!"

"You too." I stared after her for a second. Something was off. What was it?

It wasn't until I got to my car that I remembered that Shameka was walking with a little girl, and according to what she told Nicole, she had a son named Mario.

Was the girl her niece? She looked just like her.

Curiosity got the best of me, so I did some digging.

What I found made me clap my hand over my mouth in shock.

All the pictures of the little boy that were previously on Shameka's page were gone. The only pictures that contained children now were of the little girl, who Shameka confirmed was her daughter in one of the captions.

"What in the world? Whose baby was the little boy?"

I did some more digging by looking at all Shameka's family member's pages, and the little boy wasn't anywhere.

What had happened to Mario?

It could have been a hunch, but something told me my best friend had gotten played.

Chapter 53

Nicole

I was starting to get antsy. It had been two weeks since I lost my job, and none of the companies had hired me. I knew it was nothing to worry about since two weeks wasn't a long time, but I felt like I needed to be doing something other than sitting around the house.

I had one interview the other day and another one set up for tomorrow. The interview I already had went well. I was told I would get a callback within a day.

The next day, no one contacted me, so I called them this morning and was told the position had been filled. I was crushed to hear that news, but I still had the interview tomorrow to look forward to.

I was going to find another job, I knew it. I just needed to have patience.

I filled out a few more applications before calling it a night. Time to find something to cook for Zakari. I looked at the clock and saw that it was five in the evening. He would be getting home any minute, and I was sure he was hungry.

I exited the office and headed toward the kitchen, but Zakari entered the house carrying takeout bags and drinks before I could cross the threshold to the room.

"Hey!" I stared at the bags. "What's all this?"

He grinned. "I got us dinner."

I walked over to take the bag of food from him. "Wow, I was just about to cook. How did you have time to get this? I thought you got off at four thirty?"

Zakari's grin widened. "They let us out early, so I decided to surprise you."

"Wow, well I'm certainly surprised."

"Pleasantly, I hope?"

"Of course."

We headed to the dining room, and Zakari sat my drink in front of me, then began pulling the food out of the bag after I set it on the table. I went to the kitchen to grab us some plates and utensils.

I fixed the plates while Zakari sat down and took a sip of his drink.

We said grace, then dug in. The pasta was delicious, and the pink lemonade Zakari got for me had just the right blend of sugary sweetness and lemony sour.

I couldn't have asked for better.

By the time I finished eating, I was stuffed, but Zakari pulled out chocolate mousse cake for dessert, and I was done for.

"You're trying to fatten me up, and I don't like it," I teased. "A few more meals like this, and I won't be able to fit into my wedding dress."

Zakari chuckled. "I love a woman with a little meat on her bones. Besides, you only wear your wedding dress once, but you gotta eat every day."

"Can't argue with that!" I giggled, then took another bite of cake. It was divine.

Chapter 54

Nicole

I had to force myself out of bed the next morning for my interview. Good thing my eyes popped open at the right time because I slept through both of my alarms.

I had only been joking with Zakari the night before, but maybe I was putting on some weight. That was the only reason I could think of for being so tired lately.

It could also be my depression, but hopefully today's job interview would resolve that.

I got there within five minutes of the interview's start time, which was unlike me. I usually got there at least twenty minutes early so I could acculturate myself to the environment and make a good impression. So much for that.

I said a quick prayer in my car, then headed inside.

The Lord knew just what I needed because guess who the hiring manager was?

One of my friends from college, Colleen!

"Hey, Colleen!" I greeted her with a hug. "It's so good to see you."

She smiled. "It's good to see you, too. Girl, I was so happy when we pulled your application because I know you are about to be a great asset with your skillset."

That comment warmed my heart. At least some hospital was willing to see my passion for the type of work I did.

We entered Colleen's office, and I sat down across from her.

"Let's get right into it," she said. "What brings you to Lansing Hospital?"

I smiled, then launched into an explanation of my interest in the institution and my level of expertise.

I left that interview knowing I got the job.

Colleen and I had a great time catching up afterward, too, and that was the icing on the cake. I didn't want to assume she would tell me anything before they went through their other candidates, but I expected a callback for sure.

Shareese

Nicole still wasn't answering my calls, but that actually worked out for the better because I needed more proof that something was up with the whole Shameka/Jerron situation before I brought it to her.

She had been so hurt and confused by what happened, I needed something undeniable to show her what the deal was.

Confronting Shameka was my best option.

I searched her page to find out where she worked, then went to the company website for more information. Surprisingly, but happily for me, they not only had Shameka's name and photo, but they also had her position within the company. She was a receptionist, and the office was small, so it was likely she worked regular hours.

I pulled up at four o'clock in the afternoon just to be safe, and she walked outside fifteen minutes later. I wasted no time approaching her.

"Hey!" I said with a smile, and she was startled when she saw me.

"What are you doing at my job?" she asked, looking suspicious. She glanced at the office door.

"Oh, it's no worries." I held my hands up to let her know I wasn't a threat. "I just had a few questions for you."

She scrunched up her face. "A few questions for me? Girl, what is this? You're giving me weird vibes."

"Trust me, it's nothing crazy." I launched right into it. "Listen, I know you used to date my friend's ex, Jerron. As you probably know, they're broken up now, but what I wanted to know was, why did you lie to her and tell her you had a son with him?"

Shameka looked taken aback. "What are you talking about?"

I took a step closer to her and gave her a look to let her know I meant business. "I know you lied, Shameka, and all I need you to do is confess."

"Confess what? And why would I do that, anyway?"

I cut to the chase. "Your supervisor, Sandra? She's my aunt."

Shameka's jaw dropped, and I continued.

"I could send her evidence of what you did right now, and you will be out of a job."

Her eyes raced back and forth. "You can't do that. What evidence do you have, anyway?"

"Pictures from your page of your alleged son. Plus, my best friend Nicole's testimony when she finds out what you did."

"Those pictures are gone," she shot back, but then she froze as she realized I caught her.

"See how easy that was to confess?" I smirked. "Now, all I need you to do is record it on video."

"Why are you doing all this?" she sputtered. "Your friend is that pressed for a man?"

"My friend was engaged to her man of seven years before you tried to get in between them. Were you that pressed over an ex?"

Shameka sighed. "Look, I don't have time for this. I have to get back home to my daughter. What do you want from me?"

"A full confession on video, and an explanation of why you did what you did."

She was caught between a rock and a hard place, I could tell, but I wasn't leaving here without an explanation and a confession.

The story Shameka told was so crazy, I didn't believe her. Then she showed me the messages in her phone, and I was floored.

Apparently, someone named *Zaleek Muhammad* had reached out to her randomly one day, asking if she wanted to make some money. She brushed him off at first, calling him a scammer and threatening to report his page. Then he proceeded to send her a long message of his plan, pictures of Jerron and Nicole, and a promise to pay five thousand dollars for her services.

Shameka sent a laughing emoji and asked for twenty-five hundred up front. He asked for her payment app info and sent the money within seconds. He promised to pay the rest when the deal was done.

Shameka followed through, and Zaleek sent the rest of the money. Case closed.

"Where did he get the pictures of Mario, though?" I asked.

Shameka looked ashamed. "Honestly, that part is even crazier. He sent me the pictures to post on my page, and I asked the same question. He told me over the phone that he used a reversed-aging app to convert Jerron's face back to what he probably looked like as a child, then photoshopped his face onto a random kid's pictures."

"Wow." I was speechless after that.

This was unbelievable, especially when Shameka said Zaleek contacted her again after Jerron's accident asking for another favor. This time, he paid her one thousand dollars to show up at the hospital and pretend to be Jerron's doting girlfriend in front of Nicole.

He had it scheduled down to the time Nicole would arrive to see him.

"It's crazy that you went through with this, but I guess it's more power to you since you came up six thousand dollars." I gave her a look of disgust so she would know exactly how I felt about her actions.

"I needed the money," Shameka said, her lip quivering. "My baby father doesn't do anything for us."

That was no excuse, but I was done with this conversation. "Thanks for the confession," I said, rolling my eyes. "Your job is no longer in jeopardy."

I turned toward my car, and Shameka called back out to me.

"Wait, how do I know that for sure?"

I smirked, then turned back around to face her. "Because Sandra's not my aunt. I got her name from your company's website."

As I drove home, I wracked my brains to try to figure out who Zaleek Muhammad could be, and why he would go so hard to break up Nicole and Jerron's engagement?

Then it dawned on me.

Zaleek was a fake name, just like Mario was a fake kid.

And there was one person who would benefit from Nicole and Jerron breaking up.

It had to be Zakari.

Chapter 55

Nicole

I was sitting on pins and needles for four days after my interview with Colleen, especially after one by one all the rest of the positions I applied for at other hospitals were filled. This last job had to be the one.

I knew I shouldn't be worrying about this right now, especially since my wedding was less than two weeks away, but I felt like I needed some kind of vindication after all I had gone through.

Finally, my phone rang with an unknown caller. "Hello?" I answered immediately.

"Nicole? This is Colleen."

"Yes?" My heart beat wildly. Then the change in her tone caused my insides to plummet.

"Listen, I wrestled for the past few days about whether I should place this call, and today, I gave in."

"Huh?" I was confused. What was going on?

"Nicole, if you weren't interested in working for us, all you had to do was decline the interview. Did you know I talked you up to my superiors, trying to help you get this position? Then for you to do something like that? I thought we were friends."

Her voice wavered on the other line, and my mind began swimming. What had I supposedly done? What was Colleen so upset about?

"Colleen, I don't know what you're..."

"I have to go, Nicole. I just wanted to get this off my chest. When we took classes together back in college, you were a woman of integrity. I don't know what changed about that, but girl, this is not a good look."

"Colleen, what did I supposedly do?"

She sighed as if she were exasperated. "The email you sent my boss."

"Email? What email? I never sent any email, Colleen."

"I had my guy in IT check the IP address, because I didn't believe you would do such a thing, even though it came from the same address you supplied in your application, but you did. I'm so disappointed that this happened. Now my higher ups are looking at me like I'm crazy for recommending you to them."

"Colleen, I swear..."

"I gotta go." She hung up before I could say another word.

What email was she talking about? I raced to Zakari's office and pulled up my account, scouring the inbox and sent folders. There was no email. I even checked the spam account and deleted messages, and nothing was there.

I had no idea how this happened, but I needed to figure it out.

Shareese

I pulled up to Zakari's house, and thankfully, Nicole's car was parked outside, but Zakari's wasn't.

"Perfect," I said to myself and drove up the long driveway.

I rang the doorbell, and it took a few moments for Nicole to answer it. Her face was tearstained like she just finished crying.

"What do you want?" she asked in a deflated tone.

"Nicole. I tried to call you several times, but you haven't been answering your phone. I don't know what that's about, but I need to tell you something."

"I haven't been answering your calls because you're a snake."

I snapped my head back. "A snake? What are you talking about?"

She crossed her arms, anger etched across her features. "What you really did with Jerron, and what you tried to do with Zakari. I know everything, so don't try to deny it."

I was taken aback. "Nicole, I told you what happened with Jerron, and you told me you weren't bothered by it. What did I supposedly do with Zakari?"

Just the mention of his name confirmed for me that he was the one behind this. Whatever lie was about to come out of her mouth, I had something for it.

"You know what you did, so there's no need to go over it. I'll still show up for your wedding since I already paid for the dress, but just so you know we're no longer friends."

The finality in her tone threw me for a loop.

"We're no longer friends? After one allegation from a man who is clearly lying to you about what he's been doing?"

She sighed. "I don't have time for this, Shareese. I have too much going on. Plus, my own wedding to prepare for."

Her melodramatic attitude was pissing me off. "Nicole, don't be stupid. This is the same thing you did with Jerron, and that whole situation turned out to be a lie. This is…"

She cut me off. "I gotta go. You can save your story for someone who has the time to listen to it."

She slammed the door in my face.

My best friend, my day one, the girl who went with me through hell and back, just slammed the door in my face. Over Zakari.

This meant war.

Chapter 56

Nicole

After Shareese left, I felt bad. I went back to the door to tell her to come in and to apologize for flying off the handle, but she was already gone. I didn't have the strength to go after her.

The fatigue I felt every day only seemed to be getting worse. I would have to get checked out soon if it didn't let up.

Everything that was happening was so confusing. The conversation I had with Colleen, getting fired from my job, and losing my friendship with Shareese, all back-to-back. It was too much for me.

I needed to get to the bottom of this today.

I snapped to attention and went to Zakari's office. There was something I was missing, and I was going to find it.

Colleen said the emails came from the same IP address I used to fill out the applications. This meant they had to come from Zakari's computer. I didn't want to go down a rabbit hole at the moment of the implications of that reality, so I focused on finding the alleged emails instead.

I pulled up a search bar and typed in how to recover deleted emails and added my email provider's name to the search.

After a few seconds, I found an article that explained how to find what I was looking for. Apparently, my email provider had two types of deleted folders, the trash folder, which was the one I had looked at immediately after my phone call with Colleen, and the permanent deletion folder, which you could only find by searching deeper into the system. The permanent deletion folder usually only came into play when a person had too much data being used on their account and needed to clear up space.

I found it.

And what I found on it confirmed my dreaded suspicions.

There were several emails in there. All sent to various jobs I had applied for, including Colleen's hospital. Each message was more outlandish than the last.

I honestly have no idea why I applied to this stupid company...

After leaving that uncoordinated interview, I have decided to withdraw my application...

Who hired the lady who interviewed me? She was such an idiot...

The messages went on and on.

Zakari had done this, it was undeniable. He was the only person in the house besides me. But why?

As I contemplated that question, another realization dawned.

I went back to the search bar and checked the history. I didn't need to go any further to see the sites that listed various sleep remedies. And antipsychotic pills.

That explained why I had been so tired lately. And confused. And why Zakari offered so readily to cook and to bring home food from various restaurants.

I only cooked one time so far, and as I thought back, I remembered that was the only time I didn't wake up tired the next morning.

He was drugging me and sabotaging my chances of getting jobs. Why?

Zakari had some explaining to do when he got home.

Shareese

I pored over Zaleek Muhammad's page, looking for clues that it was Zakari. I recognized the profile picture from the messages Shameka showed me on her phone. Now that I thought of it, I should have asked for screenshots, but I figured her video confession and proving that this was Zakari's page would suffice.

Unfortunately, there didn't seem to be any evidence.

From all appearances, it looked like a normal page. There were a few different types of pictures of Zaleek on the page, but I had a hunch it wasn't him.

I had a lightbulb moment. There was this show I used to watch where people used search engines to see if a person was being catfished. I tried my luck and voila! Zaleek was really Kalim Rogers. I took screenshots of that evidence, but still needed more.

I went back to Zaleek's page, then got another idea.

I looked up how to find out the source of a profile and followed the steps in the article provided.

Voila again. The email address provided was zakariidabomb@mailnex.com. Got him.

Chapter 57

Nicole

I heard the front door open and shut as I printed out the last email Zakari sent to one of my jobs. I wondered if he somehow got me fired from the hospital I was working at?

That would be another question to ask him.

I swiveled around in the seat to face him as I heard his footsteps approaching the office.

"Nicole!" he said, then forced a smile onto his face. I could tell it was fake because it didn't reach his eyes. I didn't have time to play with him, though. I immediately launched into my questions.

"What is this, Zakari?" I held out the papers, walking over and brandishing them in front of his face.

He blinked and took them from me, reading them over, then looked back at me. The expression on his face was clear this time. He was pissed.

"How did you find these?"

"The better question is, why are you sending these messages in my name? Also, I found all your searches for sleeping pills and antipsychotics. Are you drugging me?"

His eyes widened at that last part, then narrowed into slits.

He looked so scary, it caused me to take a step back. I had been so sure of myself moments prior, but now Zakari was worrying me.

I had never seen him look like this before.

"Nicole, why did you go snooping on my computer?"

"That's not the question, Zakari. The question is, why are you drugging me, and why are you sabotaging my career? Did you get me fired from my job? Did you?"

I poked him in the chest as I spoke.

Bad idea.

He grabbed my arms and roughly pulled them down to my sides.

"Let go of me!" I struggled against him, but he wouldn't let go.

I stomped on his foot to distract him then quickly pulled back. It worked, and I broke free in enough time to haul back and slap his face.

Another bad idea.

His look of fury was enough to cause me to dodge him as he grabbed at me again, then I scurried around him and fled out the office door.

I didn't get far.

Zakari wrenched one arm behind my back, then wrapped his other arm around my neck. I began to panic because his hold was too tight.

"Let me go! I can't breathe! Zakari, let me..."

I felt something sharp prick my upper left arm, and within seconds, my strength dissipated. The room went black.

Shareese

I pulled up to Zakari's house, and this time, Zakari's car was outside, but Nicole's was gone. Fine with me. Maybe I could get him to confess, too and secretly record it. I pressed the button on my phone, prepared for whatever came out of his mouth.

Zakari took a while to come to the door after I rang the bell.

His outfit was wrinkled, and he looked upset. "What do you want?" he asked.

"For you to confess your lies to my friend."

He sighed. "Nicole's not here, Shareese."

"I can see that from the fact that her car's not out front. I'll wait, though. I'm sure she'll want to hear this when she comes back."

"She's not coming back."

I stared at him. "What do you mean she's not coming back?"

"We had an argument, and she left. The engagement is off."

"Did she find out what you did? Where did she go?"

He shrugged like he was irritated by my questions. "I don't know what you're talking about because I never did anything to that woman but love her. She played me, pretending to love me while the whole time she was using me for my money. I found out the truth and confronted her. She told me she was leaving. That was an hour ago."

My eyes narrowed. "Where did she say she was going?"

He shrugged again with impatience. "I don't know, and I don't care. Probably her mother's house. Aren't you her best friend? Shouldn't you know?"

I studied him. Something wasn't truthful about the way he was acting, despite his attempts to appear bothered by my presence. "I don't know, but I will find out."

"Good for you." He slammed the door in my face.

Chapter 58

Nicole

My mind was swimming when I woke up. I was in a room I didn't recognize. I looked around and saw there was a closet and a bathroom but no windows. Fluorescent lights hung above me, and they were turned on to a low setting.

I got up and crept over to the bathroom.

Everything was silent around me.

The bathroom was set up like any normal bathroom, and it contained a shower, along with towels, tissue, toiletries, and feminine products.

"What the...?"

"Good morning, Nicole."

I almost jumped out of my skin at the sound of Zakari's voice, but he was nowhere in the room. Where was he?

I wildly looked around and saw a round fixture on the ceiling. An intercom. Oh my God.

"I have a hidden camera set up. That's how I know you're awake," Zakari said as if he anticipated my question.

"Why are you doing this?" I stammered as I gathered my bearings. "Zakari, you need to let me out of here." I looked around further, but I didn't see any doors. How did I get in here? And more importantly, how would I get out?

There were vents lining the bottom of the walls near the floor, which explained why I hadn't suffocated to death. Surely, he wasn't planning to keep me here forever, though?

Zakari's voice interrupted my thoughts. "You and I are meant to be, Nicole. I suspected you would need a little more convincing before our special day, and that's why I prepared this room for you. Don't you worry, though, you will have everything you need leading up to our wedding day."

"Zakari, I'm not marrying you. You can't make me, so you might as well let me out of here. I promise I won't tell anyone what you did. Please, just let me out."

There was silence for a few moments before he spoke again.

"I'm sorry, Nicole. I can't do that."

Shareese

The whole drive over to Nicole's mother's house, I felt like something was wrong. Zakari's attitude seemed too well-prepared. Like he'd rehearsed our conversation before we had it.

When I got to the house, of course, Nicole wasn't there. I knocked on the door anyway.

"Shareese?" she answered, looking surprised. "What are you doing here?"

"Listen, Ms. Belle. I think something happened with Nicole."

I didn't want to worry her with my deepest fears in case I was wrong about how far Zakari would go in his obsessions with Nicole, but by the time I finished explaining my case, she was ready to go with me to the police.

Unfortunately, when we got there, they barely listened to us.

"Has it been twenty-four hours?" the bored-looking clerk asked.

"No," Ms. Belle said. "But..."

"Then you'll have to wait. Fill out these forms in the meantime, then come back if she hasn't checked in by tomorrow."

Ms. Belle and I looked at each other. We both wanted to do more, but we knew they wouldn't help us until enough time passed.

Chapter 59

Nicole

I had to get out of this room and out of this house. How, though? I found the place for the door, but it was no use to me without a handle or knob. I had nothing to slide into the slit in the wall to figure out where the lock was.

Plus, Zakari already mentioned he had a camera set up to watch me, so there wasn't much I could do without him seeing me. I was trapped.

The first day, I spent most of my time trying to come up with a plan for escape. Then, I finally went to the bathroom to relieve myself, and that was when Zakari took his opportunity to bring me a meal and a change of clothes, along with pajamas.

He was gone before I could exit the bathroom.

I burst into tears when I saw the clothes and the food but no way out.

"Don't cry, babe," he said over the intercom. "I brought you a delicious meal. Check it out."

I wouldn't have wanted any food from him, except for the fact that I was starving.

I ate the meal and drank the glass of soda, then went to sleep for the night.

Of course, I woke up tired the next morning.

When I glanced at the floor, I saw that my plate of food from the previous night was gone and replaced with breakfast and a box of snacks. There was also now a dress hanging in the closet. My wedding dress.

The hanger! I could use hanger to find out where the lock was for the door. Then I would escape the moment Zakari left. He had to go to work sometime, right?

As if on cue, Zakari's voice filled the room. "Off to work, babe. I had your dress pressed yesterday. You should try it on to make sure it still fits. If not, we may need to get it resized. I left some books for you to read so you won't be bored. I'm thinking of giving you a TV, too, but only if you behave. Talk to you later. Bye!" He said his last words in a cheery voice, then had the nerve to make a kissing sound before the room went silent again.

I went over to look at everything he left for me. There was a second box next to the box of snacks. It was smaller, which was why I hadn't noticed it before. I examined the books. It was the *When The Vows Break* series by one of my favorite authors, Lakisha Johnson. I didn't bother to question how Zakari knew I liked her books.

The titles made me question if he was trying to send me a message or something. I didn't have the strength to figure it out, probably due to the sleeping pills Zakari undoubtedly included with my meal.

"Should have left *Almost Destroyed*," I said with disgust.

I glanced at the dress in the closet, then walked over to examine the hanger. It wouldn't do. It was one of those thick plastic ones. It wouldn't fit through the tiny slit in the wall that was the door frame.

Back to square one.

I sat on the floor and ate my breakfast in silence. By the time I finished, I was sure Zakari was long gone.

Sometime after I ate my breakfast, I plopped back onto the bed and started reading the first book in the series. I was a speed reader, so I would likely finish the whole set of books before the day was over, but there wasn't much else to do but pull my hair out trying to find a way of escape.

Then I got an idea. Prayerfully, it would work.

"Please, Lord," I muttered as I carried the book over to the place I knew the door was.

I slid the cover of the book through the slit in the wall and moved downward until I hit something solid.

I found the lock!

"Thank you, Jesus!" I said and pushed the cover down harder. The lock didn't budge. That didn't deter me.

I added a few pages, as many as would fit, and slid the book down again. It still didn't budge.

I tried from the bottom part of the door. Still nothing.

In exasperation, I slammed the book down through the slit as hard as I could, but all that did was rip the pages and front cover clean in half.

I let the book fall to the floor as I sank in despair.

I had to get out of this room.

Jerron

The time was finally here. Discharge day. It had felt like ages as I traveled on the road to recovery, but in reality, it was only a couple months.

I still had to do physical therapy to completely heal my arm and leg, but I was healed enough to leave the hospital.

All I could think about during my stay here was Nicole.

One of the nurses informed me that she came to visit me around the time the accident happened. That let me know she still cared, even though she hadn't come back since.

I tried to reach out to her on the messaging app, but she blocked my new profile. I asked Mike and Tina to reach out, but they said she blocked their phone numbers and pages, too. I wasn't sure whether they were lying because they wanted me to give up or if Nicole had truly given up on me.

I held out hope for the former.

The first thing I wanted to do when I left was get a ride to Nicole's apartment. I prayed she would answer the door, and if she did, I would force her to listen so I could convince her I wasn't lying about not cheating with Shameka.

She had to see the truth for what it was. It was crazy I hadn't been able to show her up to this point.

I waited for the doctor to come with my discharge papers. Mike was on his way to pick me up. I hoped he wouldn't give me a tough time when I asked him to bring me to Nicole's house. If he refused, I would use a ride service when I got home.

I got the shock of my life when the nurse entered the room, saying I had a visitor, and in walked Shareese.

My brows furrowed. What was she doing here? Had Nicole sent her? Why?

"Hey," she said.

"Hey."

We stared at each other for a moment. Me and Shareese never quite got along, and it was all my fault. Back when I was a freshman in high school, we dated briefly. After the second date, I ran into Nicole and forgot all about her. I didn't have the heart to hurt her feelings, so I disappeared on Shareese in hopes that she would get the picture.

Then when things took off between me and Nicole, she introduced me to her best friend. Shareese gave me a strange look when she saw me but didn't say anything, so I didn't either.

Then she finally confronted me, and we had a huge blow up.

The tension between us remained all the way to me and Nicole's breakup.

It was stupid, I should have told her, but I didn't want Nicole to break up with me over girl code, if such a thing existed.

"What are you doing here?" I asked to break the silence.

Shareese sighed. "Listen, Jerron. I know you're just getting out of the hospital, and I don't mean to bother you, but I think Nicole is missing."

That got my attention. "Missing? What do you mean, missing?"

I listened as Shareese told me one of the most convoluted stories I ever heard.

Chapter 60

Shareese

The police investigation was finally underway. At first, they still weren't trying to let us file the report, despite the fact that twenty-four hours had passed since Nicole disappeared, but when Ms. Belle threatened to call the news stations and file a discrimination lawsuit, they stopped being jerks and began the case.

The first thing they did was check Nicole's cell phone records for the last phone call and last tower she pinged. Her final location was on a highway before the records ceased. When I heard that, I knew Zakari had done something to her.

I hoped it wasn't what I feared.

Jerron

This whole situation was bizarre. Nicole wasn't the type to up and disappear, so I was with Shareese on her theory that Zakari had done something to her.

If he did the worst, I would kill him.

I was calling the detective every few hours for updates, even though he told me he would call me when he had a lead. I didn't care. I needed more than ever for Nicole to be okay. Even if she decided not to hear me out or take me back, she didn't deserve any harm done to her.

Finally, the detective called my phone with some news.

My ears perked up when he said it, but my heart sank when I heard what the latest development was. Ms. Belle, Nicole's mom, had contacted the news stations, and search teams had gone out to try to find Nicole.

They didn't have to look far.

Her car was found in a wooded area just outside the city.

Inside the front passenger's seat were pieces of her destroyed cell phone, her purse, keys, and wallet, and a handwritten note declaring that she was going away for a while and would be back soon.

Ms. Belle, Shareese, and I knew Nicole didn't write that letter, but to the news stations and detective, this was enough evidence to close the case.

"I know it's tough to hear, but things like this do happen," the detective said. "She did leave the note, so it's likely she will come back as promised. Just be patient and allow her to sort out her thoughts and feelings, like she said. She'll come around."

His tone was nonchalant, like he didn't care whether Nicole came back and wanted to get on to his next case. I wanted to go to that station and crush his face.

Chapter 61

Nicole

I felt like I was losing my mind with each day that passed by me.

Zakari finally brought a TV into my room while I slept one night, and my hopes were lifted when I saw the news story about my disappearance.

They had search teams and everything, and I prayed the police would come and question Zakari and that he would let something slip.

He hadn't let on that they had questioned him yet, so I was banking on it happening at any moment.

Then my soul deflated when I saw the breaking news that my car was found with an alleged note I had written saying I was running away. The letter said I was depressed over losing my job and friendship with Shareese, and with being turned down for recent positions I had applied for, so I needed *a few moments away to clear my mind.*

I sucked my teeth when I heard that.

I had written no such note, and to make matters worse, I didn't even talk like that!

Zakari had done this, but how did he make the letter look like I had written it?

I asked him that night after he brought my meal.

He always brought my meals when I went to the bathroom. I tried hard to hold my bladder after he announced he had come home from work, so I could confront him face to face.

Unfortunately, it didn't work because it got so bad, I was about to pee myself. I gave in, and of course, Zakari put the food in the room and was gone before I could get off the toilet.

He spoke to me over the intercom while I was eating, and I swore he was taunting me.

"Nicole, you really shouldn't hold yourself like that. You don't want to have to wear diapers when we're older."

"How did you manage that letter?" I asked, cutting to the chase. "You and I both know I didn't write it."

"I didn't, either," he said as if making casual conversation. "Rasheeda did it."

My jaw dropped. "Rasheeda?" Rasheeda was the woman who had taken over my apartment after I foolishly agreed to move in with him.

"Yeah, she's actually an artist and handwriting expert. I told her I was working on a project for a class I was taking, and she offered to do it for me for a few bucks."

Realization dawned. Zakari's plan to force me to marry him went much further than I had imagined. If he already had Rasheeda at his beck and call, what else had he done? How far did he go in his plans?

I needed a way out and fast.

"Zakari," I started since he appeared to be in a talking mood. "How are we going to get married if you have me locked up in this room? We need to get to the courthouse sooner or later."

"That's actually something I wanted to talk to you about," he responded.

My ears perked up.

"We don't need some silly officiant to give us permission to take our vows. I did a little research on

Self-Solemnization, and it turns out, we can marry ourselves! Isn't that great?"

"Self-Solemn... What? I'm pretty sure that's not legal, Zakari."

"It is," he said in a gleeful tone. "All it will take is a quick trip to Wisconsin, and we're good. I already got our license."

I didn't bother to ask how he got our license without my signature. My guess was that Rasheeda had struck again.

Zakari continued. "I know you're wondering how we'll get there without anyone noticing. Don't worry about that, I've already thought of everything. We'll leave at night, and you'll be asleep, so the lengthy trip won't be a problem. By the time you wake up, we'll be there, get it done, then come back home. We'll do it next weekend."

The days were closing in on me. I needed a solid plan soon.

Shareese

Zakari probably had Nicole trapped somewhere, I knew it. Probably in that obnoxiously large house he lived in that the police refused to search.

They questioned him during the first couple days of Nicole's case, but he didn't present himself as suspicious.

When her car was found with that note in it, they didn't lift another finger in his direction.

He wasn't going to get away with this, I swore. I would catch him if I had to, but how?

Jerron was wracking his brain for ideas just like I was. So was Ms. Belle. She didn't believe Nicole had left on her own accord, either, but none of us had proof Zakari had her, even after showing them the fake page he created for Zaleek Muhammad and the lengths he had gone to trick her into thinking Jerron cheated.

They shot down every idea we had, all because of that note.

"She said in the note she broke up with Zakari, and Zakari's story checks out. At the time of her last cell phone ping on that highway, he was at work. We have video footage to prove it. I'm sorry, but your friend did exactly what she said in the note. Be patient. She'll be back."

They kept saying that to pacify us, but we knew they didn't care about Nicole.

As soon as they had a reason to stop looking, they took it.

It was disgusting.

Jerron called my phone as I lamented over the situation. "Hello?" I answered, hoping he had found something.

"I'm going over Zakari's house. You want to bring me?"

Chapter 62

Jerron

In my heart of hearts, I knew it was a dead end, but I had to at least try. Shareese and I pulled up to Zakari's house, and thankfully, his car was outside.

I figured if I talked to him, man to man, maybe he would give us a hint as to where Nicole was or what he had done to her.

We rang the bell, and I prayed internally the Lord would give us a breakthrough.

He answered the door eating an apple like we interrupted his afternoon snack.

"Hey... Jerron, right?" he squinted as he recognized me. "Shareese." He stared at her, then back at me.

"Zakari, we were wondering..." I started as I strained my ears for any sign or sound that Nicole was inside. "Have you heard from Nicole? Has she reached out to you since she left?"

He shook his head, then took a bite of his apple. "No, she hasn't. It's crazy that she just up and left like that, but you know how Nicole is... quick to jump to conclusions or fly off the handle. She'll probably be back soon."

The way he said that was a dead giveaway to me that he had done something. Like he was feeding us a reason to believe Nicole had really gone away on her own. I fought to maintain my composure. We had to keep it cool to keep him talking in hopes that he would let something slip.

Shareese took over. "Zakari, did Nicole say anything to you about where she might go when you guys had your argument? I know you said before that she didn't, but did you remember anything now that it's come out that she left town? Anything that might have been a clue as to where she was going?" Her eyes filled with tears. "I really just miss her."

Zakari stared at her as she spoke, not blinking and not pausing as he continued to take bites of his apple.

There was a coldness about him underneath the surface, and it set off alarm bells all through me. Zakari was more dangerous than we thought.

He waited a beat, then responded. "No, Shareese, she sure didn't. The last thing I remembered was her saying something about her mother's house, but I was so upset I barely listened."

"And she didn't pack a bag before she left, either?" Shareese pressed. "I would think she would have, since you guys had a fight."

Finally, he paused mid-bite. Something flickered in his eyes, and I caught it. He hadn't considered that question. "No, I don't think she did. She stormed out and slammed the door behind her. I'm sorry, I wish I had more information, but I really don't know what happened."

He was lying, and I knew it. The problem was, I didn't know how to break him.

Shareese

Silence consumed us as we sat back in the car. I knew in my heart Zakari was lying when he said he didn't know where Nicole was, but I had no way to prove it.

Jerron turned to me from the passenger's seat. "Did you hear any sounds in the house while he was talking?"

I shook my head. I had been straining my ears the whole time, hoping to hear a scream, a scrape, something. I guessed I watched too many movies.

Real life didn't work that way.

I turned the key in the ignition. "I just wished there was a way we could catch him up. Find a hole in his story. He can't be that good that..." I slammed on the breaks, causing Jerron's head to flap back and hit the headrest.

"What?" he asked.

I swallowed. "It's a long shot, but there's one person I know that knows Zakari better than anyone."

"Who?"

We pulled up to Lester's house a half hour later. Thankfully, there was a car outside. "Nicole said Lester got married to a woman named Michelle," I told Jerron. "Hopefully that's his car and not hers."

Jerron grunted in response, and we got out of the car to approach the door.

Just then, Lester exited the house, clicking his key fob but stopping short when he saw us. "Hey!" he said, then gave me an uneasy look. "Shareese, how are you?"

I wasted no time launching into the reason for our appearance. "I'm sure you heard about Nicole."

He stared at us and nodded. "I'm sorry about what happened."

Jerron cut in. "Hey, man, have you noticed anything strange about your friend Zakari?"

My eyes shot to him. What was he doing? He was going to scare him off!

Lester looked startled that he had asked such a question. "Who are you?"

It was at that moment I realized Lester had never met Jerron. "This is Jerron, Nicole's ex."

"Did you and Nicole get back together?" The words shot out of Lester's mouth, then he shook his head up like he had spoken too quickly. "I mean, before she left town."

Since he was already hot under the collar, I decided to continue that line of questioning. "What would make you think they got back together?"

Lester got tongue tied. "Oh... no, I just... I know him and Nicole had broken up shortly before her and Zakari got back together."

"But why would you think Nicole and Jerron were back to seeing each other? Did Zakari mention anything to you?" I took a step closer to him, and Lester started sweating. He knew something, I knew it.

"Look, guys, I'm not one to start trouble. No, Zakari didn't mention anything to me about that."

Jerron asked the next question. "Why would you think you were starting trouble? Is there something going on that we should know about?"

Lester was afraid. It was all over his face. "I'm not trying to cause any issues for my friend."

"Lester, if you know something else happened aside from Nicole leaving on her own, you need to tell us. It's the right thing to do."

Tears filled Lester's eyes, and I almost felt bad for him. He stammered as he said his next words, like it was hard for him to get them out. "Listen, I don't know if this... It probably doesn't..." He took a deep breath, then stared back at his house, then faced us. "There was a man at Zakari's house the night he said Nicole left."

Jerron cut in. "A man? Who?"

"What did you see, Lester?" My fingers found the record button on my phone just in case he tried to renege on his story. I pressed it as he continued.

Lester swallowed, then looked at Jerron. "I went there to shoot the breeze with Zakari since my wife was having a girl's night. I was about to pull down the driveway when a man pulled out of Zakari's garage, driving Nicole's car. I thought he was you, Jerron. I had never met you before. When I went to the house, Zakari told me he and Nicole broke up, so I thought that was confirmation. Then... on the news... I didn't know what to do."

"You didn't tell this to the police?" I was so heated; my ears were steaming.

He stammered. "They never came to question me. I thought..."

"You could have gone to them," Jerron said.

Lester wrung his hands. "I know. I'm sorry. I just... I didn't know what to do, and I didn't want to get Zakari in trouble in case he really hadn't done anything."

"But you suspected that he might have?" I questioned, my tone slicing through the air.

Lester winced as if I had slapped him.

His eyes shifted.

Jerron cut in again. "Lester, if there is anything else you know, anything at all, you need to tell us now. We don't know what kind of danger Nicole is in or if she's even still alive."

When Jerron said that I knew we had him.

Lester wiped his forehead to stop the sweat from getting to his eyes. "I might know something."

"What is it?" I said in the calmest voice I could muster. "Whatever it is, you can say it. We just want Nicole safe."

"Besides, if something does happen, her blood is on your hands," Jerron finished.

I felt like he should have kept that part to himself, but Lester gave in. He pulled out his phone. "I took this a long time ago," he started. "Before Zakari's house was built. He was showing me the floor plans. It's just a draft, not the finished copy, but I thought it was strange, even then. I took this picture when he went to the bathroom."

"What is it?" I asked, and he scrolled through his phone, the discomfort evident on his features. It took him a minute, but he found what he was looking for, then held it out to us. It was a picture of a floorplan, as Lester described, but there was a secret room to be installed in the house between the dining room and kitchen.

I studied the picture, then looked back up at Lester. "And you had this the whole time?" I texted the picture to my phone before he could say anything, then thrust his phone back into his hands. "You better hope nothing happened to my friend!" I barked. "She better still be alive!"

Chapter 63

Nicole

Today was the day. I had a plan of escape, and it was going to work.

Zakari came home from work and announced his presence through the intercom as usual. I pretended to be holding back my bladder again by squishing my legs together and squirming around like I had to pee.

After a while, I faked like I had given up and went to the bathroom, closing the door behind me, but leaving it slightly cracked so I would hear exactly when Zakari entered the room.

Like clockwork, the room door opened, and I wasted no time, bursting through the bathroom door and charging at Zakari like a linebacker.

I caught him off guard, so I was able to knock him to the ground, but I had to move quickly. I scrambled to my feet as he did the same, then it was on. I ran through the bookcase in the dining room and out through the kitchen. Zakari was hot on my heels, but I wasn't giving up until I was out the door. I was in the living room, halfway to my freedom when a pair of strong arms yanked me up from behind.

"No!" I screamed and struggled against him with all my might, but he was too strong. He wrapped his arm around me in a sleeper hold. I had to think quickly. I grabbed a lamp from the end table next to us and tried to swing it to hit him in the head but kept missing. I was losing consciousness fast, so I hurled the lamp at the living room window. It shattered, and Zakari swore under his breath. I continued to struggle against him until I lost consciousness.

Shareese

Jerron and I went over what Lester told us after leaving his house.

"What do you think we should do?" I asked him, my mind racing with possibilities.

"I want to go over there and bust her out," Jerron replied. "But I think we should go to the detectives first. They have to listen to us now."

Unfortunately, that was a waste of time.

Detective Michaels listened politely to our story and my recording of Lester's recounting of what happened, then sighed.

"You guys are going to have to give this up. For the last time, your friend went out of town. We can't afford to waste police resources on someone who's not truly missing."

"But you see the floorplan right here!" I thrust it in his face.

"No, we see a draft of a floorplan, as Lester said in the recording. Did he give you permission to do that, by the way? See where I'm going with this?"

Jerron tried next. "Detective, you don't think there's anything at all suspicious about this? What about the fact that Lester said he saw a man driving Nicole's car? That could be a sign of foul play, can't it?"

Detective Michaels gave him a polite smile. "Yes, I'm sure it could, but you're forgetting the note we have in Nicole's handwriting, which our office analyzed for authenticity."

"But Zakari never mentioned a man coming to the house to pick up her car. Come on, Detective!"

"Again, that's nothing but hearsay, and from a recording you captured illegally. The case is closed, guys. Sorry I can't be of further assistance."

He wasn't sorry at all, and we knew it.

We went to Ms. Belle's house next and told her what Lester told us. "That dirty dog!" she thundered, then forced herself to calm. She took a few deep breaths, then faced me and Jerron. "Okay, you two, here's the plan. We're going to get my baby back ourselves."

Chapter 64

Lester

I was a trainwreck after that conversation with Shareese and Jerron. I knew I should have gone to the police as soon as I saw on the news that Nicole was missing, but I didn't do it out of loyalty to Zakari.

Now I feared that my actions caused more harm than good.

I had to make this right.

I showed up to Zakari's house, not sure what I was going to say to him, but I knew I had to say something. If he had done something to Nicole, maybe he would confess it to me. Zakari was my oldest friend, and I hated the idea of betraying him, but if he had done something, I couldn't have that over my head.

It was the right thing to do, like Shareese said.

When I walked up to the door, I noticed there was a black trash bag taped to the window with duct tape like it had recently been broken. That sent a chill down my spine, but I ignored it and rang the bell.

There was a long moment that passed before Zakari answered. "Hey," he said in a flat tone.

"Hey. What's with the window, man?" I nodded in the direction of the covered glass.

Zakari scowled. "Stupid kids from the neighborhood."

His words hit me like a shot to the chest. He was lying, and it should have been obvious that I would pick up on it. Zakari didn't have any neighbors around him for at least a mile. What kids would travel that far just to break his window?

"What brings you here?" Zakari asked.

"I have to talk to you about something."

His eyes narrowed. "About what?"

I swallowed. "It's Nicole, man."

He immediately grew defensive. "What about her?"

I held my hands up to calm him. "Relax, I just wanted to ask about her."

"What do you want to know about Nicole? And what could I possibly tell you that the police haven't already shared with the public?"

I cut to the point. "Zakari, I know you didn't tell them the whole story." I leaned into him when I said that, trying to gain his trust in hopes that he would open up to me.

Something flashed in his eyes. "What are you talking about?"

"I saw a man drive her car out of your driveway the night she disappeared."

Zakari froze, then tried to play it off. "What are you talking about, Lester? You didn't see anybody."

"Yes, I did, Zakari. He was wearing a black hoodie, and his hair was twisted in locs."

He remained calm. "Lester, I'm not sure what you think you saw, but why don't you come in so we can talk about it?"

I relaxed. Zakari stepped aside, then I walked in, and he closed the door behind me.

"You know, man, we really don't have to..." My voice trailed off, and the color drained from my face as I looked back at Zakari to see a gun pointed in my direction.

I held my hands up, my body coursing with fear. "Zakari, whoa, what's going on, man?"

"You tried to set me up," he said in a menacing tone.

"What are you talking about?" I stared at the gun then at him. He smirked.

"That detective who was working on Nicole's case came here an hour ago. He told me it was probably nothing, but he started asking about a man driving Nicole's car that night. He said that someone mentioned they saw him. When he said that, I thought who could that someone possibly be? Then you showed up, answering my question."

I stammered. "Look, Zakari, you don't have to do this. We're boys!"

"Until you crossed me!" he spat.

"Zakari, wait!"

"Sorry, Lester," he said, then pulled the trigger.

Michelle

It wasn't like Lester to not answer his phone, especially at a time like this. He called me and told me he was going to the police about what he saw that night at Zakari's house.

I had been trying to get him to do it since he told me, but he was stubborn.

"It's probably nothing, Michelle," he kept saying. "Besides, what if I get him in trouble with the police, then Nicole randomly shows up like she said she would in that letter? He could lose his job, he could go to jail, anything could happen. We need to wait this out."

I didn't know what happened to change his mind until he told me that Shareese and Nicole's ex, Jerron, had come by.

He sounded spooked out, and now he wasn't answering his phone. I hoped he hadn't gotten himself arrested.

I shook my head at that thought. Maybe he was still at the station talking to the police.

I drove by there, just to see, and went around the parking lot three times. Lester wasn't there. Then I thought to track his location.

I didn't know why I hadn't thought of that before.

My heart raced when I saw Zakari's address pop up. Lester went to see Zakari? Why?

I was on my way over there before I could think straight.

I pulled up in Zakari's driveway, but Lester's car wasn't there. Zakari's garage doors were closed, though, both of them. I swallowed as I thought of the fact that Lester's car could be in there.

No turning back now. I rang the bell, my heart beating so wildly it reached my ears. Zakari answered, and he looked normal. I would have felt stupid for coming all the way out here, if it wasn't for the fact that my husband's location pointed to this house.

"Michelle?" Zakari scrunched his face up. "What's going on? Why are you here? Where's Lester?"

He looked worried. Why was he jumping to conclusions so quickly? Something was up. I played it cool.

"That's the same question I was going to ask you. You haven't heard from him?"

Zakari shook his head. "Not today."

I was about to open my mouth and tell him it was funny he said that because Lester's location showed that he was here, but I tried another route instead.

"Let me call him again. Hold a second."

I pulled out my phone, and Zakari stared at me as I went to Lester's name in my contacts.

I called his phone, and it rang, like it had all the other times. I was about to say something to Zakari when I froze mid-sentence. There was a buzzing sound coming from the grass in front of Zakari's house. I crept over to it and saw my picture flashing up at me from Lester's phone on the ground.

My body grew hot and cold as I turned back to face Zakari. "What did you...?"

I didn't get to finish my sentence. I was staring down the barrel of a gun.

"Sorry, Michelle," he said.

"Zakari, no!"

Chapter 65

Zakari

Why was all this happening? I paced back and forth, covering my ears with my hands, trying to stop my mind from racing. Nothing was going according to plan. I didn't want to do that to Lester or Michelle, but they forced my hand.

I felt like the walls were closing in on me.

I didn't understand.

It was prophesied. Me and Nicole were meant to be. Why was the devil fighting us so hard?

We needed to get married before next weekend. That was our only option. Once we were married, Nicole would calm down and see what life as my wife had to offer.

If she still didn't agree, I would grant her a divorce.

But she would see, I knew it.

I sent an email to my job, telling them I was coming in tomorrow but needed the next few days after that off. I hated doing this at the last minute, but desperate times called for desperate measures.

I tossed and turned for over an hour trying to get a good night's sleep, until I finally gave in and took one of Nicole's sleeping pills.

I slept like a baby after that.

Shareese

We couldn't take action until after five in the evening because I needed my mom to watch my son. I hoped this process went smoothly and it wouldn't cause any harm to the new baby in my belly. Vance would kill me if he found out what I was up to.

So far, I had been able to keep him in the dark about what Jerron and I were planning. He was busy working two jobs, anyway, so he never thought to question my erratic schedule, stalking Zakari and running back and forth to the police station in pursuit of leads on my best friend's disappearance.

He held me when I cried at night, but I wiped my own tears in the morning before pressing on to find Nicole.

Today had to be the day.

Everything was in place. Me, Ms. Belle, and Jerron, were going to take Zakari down once and for all.

Five o'clock finally came, and I dropped Benny off with my mom. "Girl, are you going out with your hair like that?" She stared at me like I was crazy.

I forgot I told her me and Vance had a date night.

My mother was another person I was keeping in the dark. She wouldn't want me involved in Zakari's takedown for obvious reasons, while Vance would be worried about not just me but our baby. I prayed God would protect us both.

Me and Jerron pulled up in the woods near Zakari's house. It was a spot that gave us a direct line of sight to his home but hidden enough so he hopefully wouldn't see us. Ms. Belle was parked in another section of the woods.

We had no idea if our plan would work, but we prayed we would have a window of time where he would leave the house.

It was a long shot, but I had driven by here a few times at night when Nicole first disappeared to see if Zakari had a pattern. Some nights he would leave for at least an hour, while other times it was a much shorter timeframe.

God must have heard our prayers. Around seven, Zakari walked out of the house and went to his car.

"Thank you, Lord," I breathed.

We watched as he backed down the long driveway, then headed down the street. I turned to Jerron.

"We might not have much time."

He nodded, and we got out of the car. "Let me take the lead, Shareese," he said with a concerned expression. He was trying to protect me as a woman, but I didn't need Jerron's protection. I had a razorblade for Zakari if it came to that.

We crept up to the house in as speedy of a fashion we could muster.

To our surprise, one of his front windows was broken. I prayed he didn't have an alarm. Jerron went up to the window and ripped the black plastic bag that was holding it shut, then felt around for a way to unlock it. His eyes lit up when he found it, then he slid the window up and hoisted himself inside the house.

"Oh, Lord, please be with us!" I was starting to sweat.

Jerron opened the front door, and we were in the house.

Why didn't Zakari's alarm go off? Did he not have one? He had to with a house this big. I prayed it wasn't a setup. Maybe Zakari had seen us outside and planned this, and he was really lurking in the shadows, waiting to pounce...

I shook off those thoughts, pulling out my cell phone so I could look at the floor plans again. I only made it as far as the front door of Zakari's house before, so I hoped the room Nicole was hidden in was easy to spot.

It wasn't.

Of course, it wouldn't be. That was why it was called a secret room, right?

Zakari's dining room looked regular, as well as his kitchen. I saw no doors that could have led to a secret room. We knew it was there, though.

"Nicole?" Jerron called out. "Can you hear me? Nicole!"

We didn't hear anything.

Tears welled up in my eyes, but we had to find my friend. We had to.

I stared at the huge bookshelves that filled an entire wall on one side of Zakari's dining room.

"Wait a minute..." I said. "I know he did not!" I ran to one of the bookshelves and started pulling down books, throwing them to the floor in anger.

Zakari was never a reader. Nicole told me that in high school. I hoped I wasn't wasting my time and that he hadn't suddenly picked up an interest in literature in college.

Jerron stared at me. "What are you..."

His voice trailed off when I grabbed a book from the middle of one of the shelves, only it wasn't one book. The whole section of books was pulled forward when I grabbed that one. Jerron caught on that it was a fake set of books and took over. He grabbed it and pulled it aside, tossing it to the floor to reveal a black button in the center of the wall.

Nicole had to be in there.

I reached around him and pushed the button, tired of wasting time.

The middle bookshelf began to move. It was like a scene from a movie. The shelf crept open like a door, revealing a short hallway, then another door with a lock on it. Nicole had to be inside there.

Jerron and I ran to the door. "Nicole! I screamed at the top of my lungs. "Nicole!"

I pressed my ear to the door, but I couldn't hear anything. I knew my friend was in there, though.

We had to find a way in.

"Let me go see if the coast is still clear," Jerron said as I pulled out my razorblade. I was picking this lock one way or another.

He left, and I went to work on the lock.

A few seconds later, Jerron's voice hissed and made my hair stand on end.

"Shareese, we have to hurry! He's back!"

Chapter 66

Jerron

We didn't have much time.

Shareese was at the secret door trying to pick the lock while I was keeping watch for Zakari. I should have brought a weapon, but I wasn't thinking.

We already closed and locked Zakari's front door when we walked in, but I realized at that moment the window I climbed into was still wide open, not to mention the ripped trash bag.

Zakari got out of his car, and I immediately heard his phone ring. That had to have been Ms. Belle. She was supposed to be on standby for us.

Thankfully, he answered, and while he was distracted, I walked over to the window to shut it. He might still notice the bag, but it was the best I could do.

"No, Ms. Belle, this is not a good time..." he was saying, but she must have made him feel guilty because he didn't hang up on her.

"Shareese, how are we looking?" I called out in a yell-whisper.

"Still trying!" she yell-whispered back. "The razorblade was too big, so I'm using a bobby pin."

Razor blade? Seemed like Shareese was more of a gangster than I would ever be. She was out here picking locks and carrying weapons while I was standing here looking like an idiot. What was my place in this situation? Ms. Belle was handling Zakari on the phone, from the sounds of it, she had him praying, and Shareese was picking the lock. What was my part?

Ms. Belle

It was a miracle that Zakari answered my phone call, much less entertained a conversation with me. I played the role of a distraught mother searching for answers about her daughter. It wasn't totally an act because I was distraught, but I had to do everything in my power to keep Zakari on that phone so Shareese and Jerron could get my baby.

I knew with my soul she was in that house. If push came to shove, I would go in there and get her myself. Zakari wasn't stopping me.

He was lucky I was granting him this phone call.

I prayed a long-winded prayer, and Zakari sat through the whole thing. Seemed like he still had some religion in him, regardless of how corrupted it might have been.

After I finished praying, I still didn't see my baby walking out of his house, so I asked Zakari to say his own prayer.

Unfortunately, that plan didn't work. He only prayed for thirty seconds before saying he had to go.

I hung up with him and hoped for the best.

Chapter 67

Jerron

It was showtime. Shareese still wasn't done with the lock, so in the meantime of keeping one eye on the door and the other on her, I grabbed one of the steel pokers from Zakari's fireplace, ready for action.

Zakari started toward the front door, then stopped short.

I stared at him intently, trying to figure out his deal.

He turned and started walking in the direction of his garage. My neck craned as I saw him walk past it, then reach in his pocket and kneel.

What was he doing?

He pulled something out of his pocket, then opened the door to an underground shed and stayed in position for a few moments.

Wait… was Nicole in the shed?

Maybe me and Shareese had gotten it all wrong.

I was out of his front door before I had a chance to think. It was me versus Zakari now. No turning back.

His back was to me, so I had the advantage.

I heard muffled voices as Zakari called out to whoever was in the shed.

"I'm sorry I had to do what I did, but y'all left me no choice. I'll be back in a few days, and Nicole will be my wife. See you soon."

He closed the shed, but before he could turn around, I swung the poker and struck him in the back, knocking him to the ground.

He groaned in pain.

"Where is Nicole?" I bellowed. I knew she wasn't in the shed, but I wasn't entirely sure she was in that secret room anymore.

"Jerron?" He moaned, then started moving.

I clenched the tool, ready for more action until Zakari flipped around and whipped out a gun in one swift motion.

Just that quickly, I was on the losing end of this battle.

"Come on, Zakari, man. You don't want to do this!"

His evil smirk let me know I was wrong in my assumption. "Looks like we got another one for the shed."

Chapter 68

Shareese

In all my nervousness, I had gone through three bobby pins. I kept losing patience and breaking them in half. I had one left, so this was my only chance to save my friend.

I heard the front door open, so Jerron must have gone outside to confront Zakari.

I prayed he was okay.

"Come on, Shareese," I said, then I heard a click, just as Zakari's voice shook me out of focus.

"Who's that in my house?" he boomed.

I quickly unclicked the lock to let Nicole out, but I was met with a short hallway that led to another door. The fluffy padding that was surrounding the room gave me the answer as to why we couldn't hear her and vice versa.

The other door didn't have a lock, just a black circular button like the one on the bookcase. I pressed it and turned the handle to fling open the door just as Zakari bounded through the bookcase. Nicole came out of her room just as he came in.

He had a gun.

"Shareese..." he said with a sneer. "I should have known you would be here."

"Where's Jerron?" I asked, my eyes on the gun. I refused to show fear, though.

Nicole looked like she was scared out of her mind. "Zakari, what are you doing? Just let me go! It's over, okay?"

He shook his head. "No, Nicole, it's far from over. We still have a trip to take."

"I'm not going."

He pointed the gun at her.

"Put that down!" I yelled. "Are you really going to shoot her after going through all this trouble?"

He contemplated it for a second. "Good point." Then he pointed it at me.

"Why don't you turn it on yourself instead?" I countered.

"Shareese..." Nicole's unsteady voice sounded in my ear.

"I'd rather shoot you instead."

"A pregnant woman? You would kill me and my child?"

He flinched. I had him. Zakari might have had no problem shooting me, but an innocent baby? Maybe there was a heart somewhere in there.

His expression softened then re-hardened. "Another good argument." He pointed the gun back at Nicole.

"Freeze!"

All three of us jumped as commotion sounded all through Zakari's house. Officers with SWAT written on their vests and protective hard hats on their heads came bounding into the room.

Zakari dropped the gun and put his hands up. One of the officers glanced down at it. "A tranquilizer? Really?" He stared at Zakari in shock.

Zakari didn't respond.

Nicole and I watched as he was cuffed and read his rights, then led out to the squad car.

Chapter 69

Nicole

The rest of the night was a blur after Shareese got me out of that room.

It turned out I wasn't the only one Zakari had trapped. Lester and Michelle were found bound and gagged in the shed.

Jerron, who was found lying on the grass near it, told the officers what he had done when he woke up.

We all thought Ms. Belle was the one who called the police, and she did as soon as she saw Zakari go into the house instead of Jerron, but it turned out someone else contacted them before she did. Rasheeda.

Rasheeda was feeling guilty after putting two and two together and learning that Zakari tricked her into writing that letter by lying and saying it was for a class he was taking.

It just so happened that she had gone to the police right before we went to Zakari's house, so they were on their way there the same time we were, and they got there just in time to save us all from ending up in Zakari's underground shed.

I had no idea what he was planning to do with all of us. Surely, he couldn't keep us there forever?

Anyway, Shareese and Jerron told me everything they found out about Zakari's actions, but the one thing no one could figure out was who the man was who was driving my car the night I supposedly left town.

The police launched an investigation, and Lester, Rasheeda, and Shameka were brought in for questioning. It was a big ball of confusion, but once everything was sorted out, Shameka got off for not doing anything that was technically illegal, Lester got off because although he withheld information from the police, it was his first offense, plus Zakari kidnapped him, too, and Rasheeda's case ended with a hung jury. Half the jurors didn't believe she didn't know more about Zakari's plan than she let on, while the other half believed she was innocent.

During Zakari's trial, the police were able to track his records to find that the same person Zakari paid to drive my car and leave it by the highway was also the person who hit Jerron's car with his big truck.

Since he fled the scene after the accident, and the truck was never found, there was a dead end.

Unfortunately, the most the detectives were able to find was that the guy's name was Keno. He used burner phones for all interactions with Zakari, was paid on a payment app through a prepaid card for all their transactions, and never pinged the same towers when he used the phones.

No one had a description for him except that he wore locs and a black hoodie.

Zakari refused to give up his identity, so he was still at large.

Zakari's trial was long and arduous. He and his parents paid for a high-powered attorney, who argued that since no one was physically harmed and that the person who Zakari paid to hit Jerron was a ghost, the charges should be reduced.

He got sentenced to seven years.

Despite all that happened, I didn't want anything bad to happen to Zakari. I just wanted to never see him again.

Shareese and Vance had a small but beautiful wedding, and she gave birth to a baby girl, Alysn. Benny was their ringbearer.

Both Jerron and I got new jobs, then we finally got married in front of our friends, families, and loved ones. We often had date nights with Mike and Tina, as well as Shareese and Vance.

Lester and Michelle apologized to me about withholding information from the police. I forgave them, but just like Zakari, I wanted nothing to do with them anymore.

Life finally turned around for me.

I had my friends, I had my job, and I had my man - the right one this time.

I could finally be content.

Chapter 70

Zakari

I always had the gift of gab, so the guys in here never messed with me.

It was a minimum-security prison, anyway, since my lawyer worked out that I wasn't a violent criminal. Guess that tranquilizer gun came in handy.

It was true, I wasn't a killer, and I only used force when necessary.

"Hey, Zakari," Officer Unique said, then she winked at me and blew a kiss when no one was looking.

I winked and blew one back.

That was right, I finally found the real woman of my dreams. The Lord revealed to me that Nicole wasn't my wife like I thought. This whole time, He was setting me up to be with Unique.

The first time we locked eyes, I knew she was the one.

She told me she felt the same way as soon as she got the chance.

We snuck kisses and held hands whenever the other guards and inmates weren't looking. Those who did catch onto us didn't tell and didn't care because we weren't bothering anybody.

We were in love, and no one was stepping in our way.

I planned to make things official and propose as soon as I was released. Unique said she would wait for me. My woman was so sweet.

The more time I spent in here the more I felt like Jacob.

Jacob worked seven years for Rachel but got tricked into marrying Leah. I almost got tricked into marrying Nicole, but the Lord protected me.

Just like Jacob had to work another seven years to finally get the woman of his dreams, so did I.

Nicole was my Leah.

Unique was my Rachel.

The End

Dear Reader,

I hope you enjoyed this story. If so, check out my other Christian Romance Thriller, Not What It Seems. Priscilla and Raheem's story has stolen the hearts of many readers. Check them out to get swept up in their love… and discover who's lurking in the shadows against them.

Until next time,

Tanisha Stewart

Before you go…

If you enjoyed *Every Voice Ain't From God*, I would absolutely love to hear your feedback. Please leave a rating or review commenting on your overall thoughts.

In addition, if you would like access to exclusive updates, giveaways, and more, join my email list at tanishastewartauthor.com/contact.

God bless you, and happy reading!

Tanisha Stewart

PS: If you would like to connect with me on social media, here's where you can find me:

Facebook: <u>Tanisha Stewart, Author</u>
Facebook group: <u>Tanisha Stewart Readers</u>
Instagram: <u>tanishastewart_author</u>
TikTok: <u>authortanishastewart</u>
Twitter: <u>TStewart_Author</u>
YouTube: <u>Tanisha Stewart</u>

Not What It Seems: A Christian Romance Thriller

Sparks begin to fly between Priscilla and Raheem, but soon they will learn, all is not what it seems.

Priscilla moves across the country to escape a toxic ex who won't let her go. Her mindset is healing, but within days of her arrival, she's introduced to the sexiest man she's ever laid eyes on: **Raheem.**

When Priscilla and Raheem's eyes meet, the chemistry is immediate. One would think they are a match made in heaven, and everything will go smoothly for them.

Wrong.

Because the closer Priscilla and Raheem get to one another, the more strange things begin to happen.

Sinister things.

What has Priscilla gotten herself into?

She's locked into Raheem, and he wants her to stay, but as the song goes, **jealousy is cruel as the grave...** (*Song of Solomon 8:6*).

Check it out here: Not What It Seems: A Christian Romance Thriller

Messed With The Wrong One: An Urban Romance Thriller

We all do things we live to regret, but when you harm the wrong ones, you get what you get.

Junior cheated. Marlena is furious. She resolves to teach him a lesson. What starts as a simple act of revenge, however, quickly takes a dangerous turn.

While Marlena was busy getting back at Junior, someone else happened to be planning a revenge of her own against Marlena. The deadly kind.

Marlena finds herself in a race against time to no longer change her man. Now she has to save him. And herself.

Check it out here: Messed With The Wrong One: An Urban Romance Thriller

Everybody Ain't Your Friend: An Urban Romance Thriller

They say you should keep your friends close, and enemies closer, but sometimes reality might be the other way around...

Mia thinks her life is completely normal. She has a loving boyfriend, great and supportive friends, and a close relationship with her mother.

Things take an interesting turn, however, when she is almost run down by a car one day. Then come the messages from an untraceable number. Not to mention the heartbreaking secret that is revealed shortly thereafter.

Suddenly, everything that Mia thought was right in her life goes wrong. She has no idea why, but she needs to find out, before her secret stalker decides her time is up.

Check it out here: Everybody Ain't Your Friend: An Urban Romance Thriller

Should Have Thought Twice: A Psychological Thriller

They say to always watch the quiet ones, because you never know when they might snap.

Shatina is a young woman with a troubled past and present. She lives in the shadows of her fraternal twin sister, who sucked up all the beauty genes, her best friend, whose seductive charm will sway any boy who listens, and her cousin, who is more than a knockout, but a force to be reckoned with.

Shatina feels like she has nothing going for her but her grades and her full scholarship to a four year institution of her choice... until someone comes along to threaten that.

Shatina has faced threats before, and little does anyone know, she has gained vindication over all of her enemies, one by one. Except this last one might be a bit more of a challenge than she bargained for.

Check it out here: [Should Have Thought Twice: A Psychological Thriller](#)

Vengeance Is Mine: A Psychological Thriller

The best type of revenge is one they never see coming...

Dexter went to a party with someone he trusted, thinking he was about to have a blast. What started as a night on the town ended with Dexter's **gut-wrenching screams for mercy.** No one heard.

Mentally broken and internally scarred due to the devastation he faced, Dexter is running out of options.

Something snaps within him.

He knows what to do to ease his pain.

Six men, and six months.

Just enough time to execute justice.

Vengeance is Mine is an unputdownable psychological thriller full of twists and turns that will keep you reading until the end.

Check it out here: <u>Vengeance Is Mine: A Psychological Thriller</u>

Caught Up With The 'Rona: An Urban Sci Fi Thriller

Cordell's luck could not be any worse. A young black man, a full-time student, doing his best to give back to his community by serving as a substitute teacher, only to receive an email which stated that his job would be suspended for the next three weeks due to the Coronavirus.

Frustrated about the situation, he vents to his lifelong friend, Jerone. Shortly after their conversation begins, they are approached by Markellis, a neighborhood hustler who always tries to sell Cordell and Jerone on his get-rich-quick schemes...

But this one is different. Cordell is pressed for cash, so he convinces Jerone to go along with Markellis' proposal.

No sooner than they say yes, Cordell and Jerone are swept up in an almost unspeakable conspiracy, with less than three weeks to turn it around...

Only it's much more than just Cordell and Jerone's lives that are at stake.

Check it out here: [Caught Up With The 'Rona: An Urban Sci Fi Thriller](#)

December 21st: An Urban Supernatural Suspense

Flick is a regular guy, living a regular life, then the night of Thanksgiving came.

It all started with a conversation he had with his cousin Bru that got a little heated.

Tensions rose, but things calmed down when he went to his mother's house for the family dinner.

Little did he know, that's when his life would begin to shift in a direction that he never expected.

December 21st, Saturn and Jupiter aligning, competing belief systems… what did it all mean?
Nothing, Flick thought.
Until the first event.
Then the second.

Follow Flick's journey in this Urban Supernatural Suspense as he tries to figure out exactly what's going on.

Is he losing his mind?

Or does everything that is happening have a deeper meaning?

Check it out here: December 21st: An Urban Supernatural Suspense

Where. Is. Haseem?! A Romantic-Suspense Comedy

Ever been ghosted??

Well, Stephanie has, and it doesn't feel good.

After a series of mishaps in the love department, Stephanie meets Haseem. They seem to hit it off and the chemistry between them is steadily building. Until...

Haseem disappears.

Where did he go??
No one seems to know.
But Stephanie is determined to find out.

Follow this story of romance, suspense, and comedy as Stephanie tries to figure out how the man of her dreams could just vanish without a trace.

Check it out here: Where. Is. Haseem?! A Romantic-Suspense Comedy

Tanisha Stewart's Books

Even Me Series
Even Me
Even Me, The Sequel
Even Me, Full Circle

When Things Go Series
When Things Go Left
When Things Get Real
When Things Go Right

For My Good Series
For My Good: The Prequel
For My Good: My Baby Daddy Ain't Ish
For My Good: I Waited, He Cheated
For My Good: Torn Between The Two
For My Good: You Broke My Trust
For My Good: Better or Worse
For My Good: Love and Respect
Rick and Sharmeka: A BWWM Romance

Betrayed Series
Betrayed By My So-Called Friend
Betrayed By My So-Called Friend, Part 2
Betrayed 3: Camaiyah's Redemption
Betrayed Series: Special Edition

Phate Series
Phate: An Enemies to Lovers Romance
Phate 2: An Enemies to Lovers Romance
Leisha & Manuel: Love After Pain

The Real Ones Series
Find You A Real One: A Friends to Lovers Romance
Find You A Real One 2: A Friends to Lovers Romance
Janie & E: Life Lessons

The Quiet Ones Series
Should Have Thought Twice: A Psychological Thriller
Fooled Me Once: A Psychological Thriller
Never Saw Me Coming: A Psychological Thriller
Reap What You Sow: A Psychological Thriller
Surprise Surprise: A Psychological Thriller
The Enemy You Know: A Psychological Thriller

Standalones
A Husband, A Boyfriend, & a Side Dude
In Love With My Uber Driver
You Left Me At The Altar
Where. Is. Haseem?! A Romantic-Suspense Comedy
Caught Up With The 'Rona: An Urban Sci-Fi Thriller
#DOLO: An Awkward, Non-Romantic Journey Through Singlehood
December 21st: An Urban Supernatural Suspense
Everybody Ain't Your Friend: An Urban Romance Thriller
The Maintenance Man: A Twisted Urban Love Triangle Thriller
Not What It Seems: A Christian Romance Thriller
Vengeance Is Mine: A Psychological Thriller

Printed in the USA
CPSIA information can be obtained
at www.ICGtesting.com
CBHW071453300524
9318CB00007B/99